A TRADE OF FLESH

The Seven Hands Series:
Novella One

By: Brandyn E. Harnage Jr.

Special Thanks

This novella wouldn't be possible without the help and support of my loving wife, Jorie. Thank you for all your patience, honesty, and devotion. This series is for you.

For more information regarding the author or to inquire about upcoming works please feel free to visit the Facebook Page B.E. Harnage or the Official Website of B.E. Harnage.

Thanks and Enjoy!

CHAPTER 1

The wind raged against her body—clawing at her—desperate to snatch her free and jettison her into the clouds. Solaris repositioned, allowing the gusts to race underneath her. She whipped upward and snagged on the rope. Her grip slipped a little and then she screamed with laughter when she realized she was still hanging on. There might not be another chance before the end of the summer. She bore down harder.

No. She couldn't let it happen again.

Her grip was strong, stronger than last summer. She could maintain her position now. She could conquer the cliff. She *would* conquer the cliff.

The wind howled with anger around her. *I will not let go.*

The gust intensified and shifted to the right and caught her by surprise. She slipped further, rising upward as the wind drove against her. She squeezed with all her young might and her retreat stopped. Solaris held her grip, bone-white fingertips at the crack's edge, long black hair whipping and stinging her face, her legs independently balancing in mid-air. She glanced behind her and took note of the trajectory. If she let go now, there was a good chance her landing would be...painful.

The view of the valley from the outcropping was majestic and a secret. Her secret. She had never found a better view of the valley, even when considering Rockside Bridge over the waterfall. All the tourists went there, but they didn't know any better *because* they didn't know her spot. The view from her cliff was one to be treasured forever, but the cliff was temperamental, spiteful, and potentially murderous. Others might say it was dangerous to be there—foolish even. Not Solaris.

The wind faltered for a second, and she used that break in its efforts to drive her right hand deeper into the crack. *Not much longer.* Her fingers went deep inside a hidden ledge she didn't initially realize was there. Before she could even crack a defiant smile, the wind came back and found her cheating. It beat against her. The pattern changed, driving her down and smacking her left side into the rock, and then snatched her upward again. She rebounded so hard her left hand lost its grip. She wheezed and drew her left arm in around her aching ribs.

Green Mother! They feel broken.

Challenging was the right word, and that made it all the better. Terrain, seasonality, and environment colluded to produce winds that clashed against the rockface below and then spiraled upwards. Present moment included, this was only the third time she drew up enough courage to try and tame the beast. Only three times in three years; a true travesty. The location was just too deep into the jungle for frequent visits, and… she wasn't permitted to venture far into the jungle anyway. Then again, she wasn't supposed to do a lot of things, but having fun often required taking risks. What good was having an untamable jungle for a backyard if it was left unexplored? What good were you if you didn't try?

And just like that, it was over. She had won. The rush of wind settled, lowering her body back down to the pink crystal—a roza stone. Despite being exposed all day to the blazing sun, the pink crystal was as cool as a shady pond in autumn.

Solaris rested against the cool object, panting and looking at the distant horizon. She had proven it to herself. She might not be able to sleep on her left side for a week, but now she had her trial to present to that ornery Hadagii Elder. She would share the view with the tribe as her gift and master the wind in front of them all as proof of her bravery. She did it once; she could do it again. Then they would have to accept her as one of their own, even if her father's blood roots weren't of the tree.

Solaris analyzed the canopy far below for oncoming wind movements and assessed no new gusts were upon her. Now that victory was hers, she was allowed her small reward. The teenager crawled forward and peered over the edge, scanning the valley.

Below her was a giant mass of swirling blue—gliding mok-moks created the swirl as they sliced through the mists of waterfalls in giant circle patterns. From her perch, they looked no bigger than leaves, but up close the birds would tower over her. The largest of the species could swallow her easily, but wouldn't. Mok-moks only consumed fruit. She smiled and imagined leaping from the cliff to land on the back of one of the creatures. *They're so graceful. I wonder how it would feel to glide through the air like fish swim through water*, she thought to herself. She eyed the closest mok-mok and judged the distance. *That would be something,* she thought but then pushed the thought from her mind and rubbed her aching ribs. *Way too far down.*

Below, the wide river snaked through a sea of trees, and then cut through the nearby metropolis residing at the edge of the great jungle. The water's surface reflected rivulets of red light from the setting sun. Though darkness was taking over, she could still make out much. To the west, she could see the tall outlines of the nearby metropolis, Unikai. The tallest of the buildings blinked with red rights, warning all air traffic to stay clear. Unikai had the only operating spaceport in her province. It didn't have the most traffic, but it did bring some of the most important people. Most of the human aliens and her own people's political representatives tended to use the Unikai spaceport to travel to and from the planet. Compared to the rest of the surrounding environment, Unikai was a mecca of activity, progress, modernization, and her home when she wasn't on a break from school.

Spreading far into the east, were the thousands of scattered villages of the Urokos—the Tree People. The loose affiliation of tribes had always been resistant to adopting most modern technology and any human cultural influence, yet despite this, they were prosperous and respected. They were a fierce people, deeply religious, and experts in medicinal herbs. As a whole, they worshiped Green Mother, the goddess of the jungle, and believed she provided all they should ever need or want. Solaris knew their customs well as she was a descendant of the tribe, at least by half her bloodline. Her mother was Urokos and had been raised in the river basin below, along with her grandmother who still lived there.

To the north, mountain chains adorned the horizon, most covered with vegetation, but a few rose high enough to be capped with snowy peaks. And fewer still, cradled ancient Hadagii monasteries—keepers of ancient lore and missionaries of the Green Mother. Beyond the mountains were vast deserts—beautiful as they were inhospitable.

Movement in the river caught her attention, but the reflection on the surface made it difficult to identify the cause. She narrowed her eyes, bringing the distant action into focus. *What are they doing?* she thought.

A large string of boatmen rowed across the river on rafts. Only one group of people dared to live in such an inhospitable region; only one could live in such a place and thrive—the Urokos. Solaris had spent several summers with the Urokos, and not once had she seen even one raft cross the great river at dusk. Tree people, above everyone else, knew the dangers of the night jungle. Only some great necessity could have driven them to action in that manner. She twisted her mouth. *Mercy to those who stir the Tree People.* Her gaze drifted from the river and then over the rolling canopy again. Pin pricks of orange light began piercing the growing jungle shadow. The valley people were preparing their evening fires. She glanced at the darkening jungle and felt the tugs of a maturing wisdom whisper that she should return home. The night hunters would soon prowl, looking for a tender morsel to ease their hunger.

Another gust of wind crashed into Solaris. Black strands of her thick hair lashed out, searching for her eyes, but she closed them before they could be found. She instinctively dug into the crystalline structure and pressed herself flat against the rock so the wind would flow over her. *You can't have me today, Green Mother.* The past year of growth had added a bit more muscle to her lean frame and she took advantage of it. The young woman slung her head to the side, throwing her hair in defiance. She inhaled the warm summer air and smiled.

"Fumel, fum, fum...eyah!"

Oh no. Solaris pivoted on the crystal and scanned the brush. From her angle, the vantage point was excellent. She found the gaps in vegetation and systematically searched each one. At first, her prey was elusive, and then a dark shape rushed behind two giant fan leaves. Several paces from there, a flock of birds launched into the sky, shrieking in protest and terror. A split second later, the yellow and purple leaves of a kala bush shuttered. She traced the movement points and mapped a trajectory.

Solaris released her iron grip and bounded down the formation, leaping from one ledge to the next. She landed each jump with elegance, one after the other, and after five hops, she was sprinting across solid ground. She slipped through vegetation, pushing and pulling plants as she scanned for her brother. She plotted his course correctly and was rewarded to a sight of him hunched over in ankle deep, murky water. Between slurps, he babbled jubilantly. Drawing from past experience, Solaris understood that particular parade of noises to mean: *I've gotten into something I shouldn't have. Please protect me from myself.*

"What are you doing, Kotaris?" she asked. "What...what is tha—don't put that in your mouth!"

Kotaris paused, watching his younger sister from the corner of his good eye. What higher functioning grey matter Kotaris possessed helped him conclude Solaris would be hard pressed to stop him. A wicked grin spread across his face and he ran his tongue slowly up the fumel's back. The look on his face after, revealed the taste was less than stellar to him...but it was worth it. Well, that's not entirely true. He enjoyed the euphoric rush he associated with giving the fumel a thorough tongue scrubbing. The end of the experience —being bed-ridden and nauseated—always neglected to embed itself into his long-term memory. Kotaris was not—and would never—be a strategist...

Solaris's older brother emerged into the world a breach baby—outside of a hospital, which was customary for Tree People—and a complication led to a pinched umbilical cord. Due to lack of advanced medical support, he suffered permanent brain damage. This unfortunate turn of events hindered development of a full cognitive spectrum. Despite the significant setback, he developed his communication skills to an adequate level...as long as he didn't get too excited. Kotaris didn't usually speak more than three to four words at a time, but he never aspired to be a conversationalist anyway. He was a man of action.

And so, he spent the previous nineteen years rampaging about, shoving random objects into his mouth and shouting in elated repetitions. When Solaris's maturity surpassed her brother's—which didn't take long—she took it upon herself to watch after him. That tended to be a full-time job due to Kotaris's natural ability to seek out and destroy everything not tied down or protected by an electric current. Fumels fell under this category.

The creature croaked in her brother's clutches, its eyes bulging more than normal. Those eyes seemed to be pleading for Solaris to save it. *By the good of the Green Mother, get me away from this man.* Solaris tried to snatch the yellow animal from Kotaris's clutches, but her elusive brother twisted away, placing the frog just out of her grasp. He cut his eyes at her as if she had tried to take his favorite toy. Then he licked the amphibian, and yelled "Fumel," before smothering it with his tongue again.

Give me the damn fumel! She reached out a second time only to be shut down by a practiced and stern forearm parry. The teenager sprawled backwards amazed at how little effort he seemed to use. Solaris wasn't the only one growing stronger. *I'll need to mention this to Father when we get home,* she thought. Solaris wasn't sure what his response would be, but she knew they needed to start taking extra precautions. Kotaris was already large with no sign his growth would stop soon. The combination of his unfortunate nature, strength, and curiosity was a recipe for a catastrophic situation.

"Fumel!" Slurp.

"Kotaris! I've had enough. Give it to me," she demanded.

She attempted several more rescue attempts which ended with her screaming in frustration. Tired of his games, she leapt onto his back, slipping one arm around his neck and the other over the top of his shoulder to grab the creature. Her reach was long, but not nearly long enough.

"Give it to me! Quit! Give me the— ahhhhhhhhhhhhhhh," she said, as Kotaris bolted down the slope laughing and maniacally romped through the woods. He always ran like an automaton—rigid and right through everything. Solaris noticed a flash of yellow and turned her attention to it. At the peak of his right arm pump, she could see the reluctant abductee reach out with its front legs, little fingers spread open. What the fumel was grabbing for, she wasn't sure—probably anything it could.

They flew by trees, narrowly avoiding the trunks, but found themselves being pummeled by brown and green blurs. Three times on the way down, she spat leaves out of her mouth. In between sprinting and side-stepping trees, the young fah'dienh shouted "Fumel" in his deep voice and licked the creature. Solaris clung to him with terror-fueled strength—his speed and stupidity were great enough to rocket them right over the edge of a cliff. Add to that, thick vegetation blocking sight beyond three feet, and an inevitable catastrophe was imminent.

As they raced down the slope, she imagined them going over a cliff, Kotaris pumping and running all the way down. She couldn't help but smile as she visualized the scene...and then frowned when she remembered who was on the back of the rampaging muscle. Solaris cleared her mind and searched the horizon for her bearings. The wait felt cruel, though it was really just seconds before she located the direction of the setting sunlight through the trees. Using the dimming light as her anchor, she pulled up an internal map in her mind, plotted their position, and then relaxed. He was following the path toward the house, away from any cliffs. Several evasive maneuvers later, she suppressed a giggle but let a smile escape across her face. They were going to be fine.

Thunk!

The colors of the world spun together. Kotaris kept running as if he was going up an invisible wall and then they tumbled onto the damp forest floor a tangled mess. The siblings slid to a halt, the crash ending with both laughing, though not much the same. Solaris was more pleased with the outcome than Kotaris and her laughter reflected it. His laughs were choked with moans, and he rolled back and forth on the ground.

Solaris wrestled herself under control and propped up on an elbow. She shot a glance backward to find the offender. A tree had been the culprit. A limb to be precise, and it was still wobbling from the impact of Kotaris's head. The impact had been very unfortunate—for the tree anyway.

Beep-boop, interrupted her wristband.

The faceplate of the votech was cracked, scrambling the information on the display screen. She held it close to her lips and said, "Reset." Nothing happened. She repeated the process again, but the response remained unchanged. The teenager tapped the votech and tried to place a call to the house, but the wristband refused and responded with a static whine. *Great... it's busted.* Her face was screwed up into a frown, but then it melted into a large smile. *Nooooo, it's perfect! Now I can go home and sweet talk Father into getting me the new model.* She fell backwards into a mound of leaves and practiced the smile she would give him.

Her brother stopped laughing and did a monkey roll onto all fours, "Fumel?" Kotaris shuffled along the forest floor searching for the yellow amphibian. "Fumel?" he mumbled again. He stopped raking through the leaves and stood up, pointed ears drawn back, and his attention focused on the sky.

"It won't be up there, Ko," she said. Solaris rolled onto her feet and brushed herself off. *And then again, the way he was pumping his arms...*

Kotaris didn't respond. His jaw muscles tightened as he flexed his fingers open and then tightened them into a fist. He always cycled opening and closing his hands when he knew he was going to be in trouble. The tick was a sign he was very worried.

"What's wrong?" asked Solaris.

He didn't answer, only titled his head to the side for a time, and then resumed the alert position once more.

"Ko. What is it?"

"Mmmmm...metal bird...different."

"Metal bird?" Solaris asked, as she cocked

her head to hear.

Solaris closed her eyes and listened. She could hear the wind rushing past her ears, the distant roar of a waterfall, and the crisp snapping of twigs alerting them to some beast prowling in the undergrowth—but that always turned out to be some small bird. Nothing out of the ordinary. *He must be hearing things.* She almost stopped listening, but the little voice in her head told her to wait. Time eased on and then the voice was right. Her patience was rewarded with a low rumbling off toward the western sky. The growling rumble was unnatural, pulsing, and cyclical in nature. She opened her eyes. It was only a spacecraft.

"You're right, Ko. It's just a shuttle though. Nothing to be concerned about."

"No like 'em. Hide," he said and then grabbed her arm. "Hide. Bad feeling."

"Bad feeling? What's wrong with you? You've heard a thousand of them."

"Yah, bad. We go."

"It's just a shuttle, Ko. Don't be scared—ow, not so hard." He was frantically pulling on her arm at that point.

"Bad ona shuddle. Hide. Be safe."

"Okay—okay," she said, letting him lead her away from the small clearing toward denser undergrowth. Before she could utter any protest, he forced them into the closest cover he could find. Solaris hollered as the thorniest bush in the jungle got her attention. The rumble of the spacecraft grew louder as they waited, as it closed in on them. As she waited, she realized her heart was racing. Kotaris had her spooked.

"Ko, why's it bad? Why is the shuttle bad?"

"Forest quiet." He squeezed her arm a little tighter. "Bad animal make quiet. Bad animal make…make p-pain here," he finished, rubbing his stomach. "Bad feeling in tummy."

He was right. The forest's creatures were dead quiet. Not a single living thing made a noise. Nothing.

Kotaris's large hand plopped down on top of her head and forced her to the ground.

"Hey, what's with th—"

"Down. I protect," said Kotaris. "Look," he continued and pointed to an opening in the canopy.

"Look here, Ko," she said. "I think you have this backw…," and then trailed off.

A medium-sized spacecraft passed overhead, blasting down heat and exhaust. Even from its elevated position, she still had to hold up her hand to shield her eyes from the torrential wind. She had seen many of the human's ships and the one above them was some class of cargo jumper;

a craft built for limited space flight—a hop from the planet's surface to a moon. They definitely weren't designed for deep space travel or equipped to take heavy punishment. Despite that, good portions of the craft's light armored plating were charred, gouged, or worn down to bare metal. Just as it disappeared beyond the gap in the canopy, Solaris noticed the rear hatch was agape and bustling with beings. She couldn't make out what was in their hands because of the exhaust glare, but she had a horrific idea.

"Bad humans," he said and motioned toward the wristband. "Call Dad."

"I can't, Ko. It's broken. And you don't know they are bad."

He pulled her arm close, inspected the device, and tapped the faceplate. "Worky-worky." When the display refused to respond, he licked his finger and rubbed dirt from the touchscreen. "Worky-worky," he whispered. When he realized it wouldn't work, he looked at her with pleading and confused eyes.

"It's okay, Ko. We'll go home now," she said brushing a strand of hair off of his face. That's when she spotted the change in his good eye. The pupil had dilated. Kotaris grabbed a wad of his hair and pulled it back down over his face.

"Light...bright," he said grinning. "Funny colors." Kotaris looked down at her and grabbed the pendant around her neck. He turned it over in his hand, and his eyes widened.

What light, she thought, glancing at the sky. "You...you are just you," she said. Solaris gave a nervous chuckle, took his hand in hers, and led them down the slope toward their home. She guessed the effect would wear off fairly quickly due to his resistance from previous self-indulgences. And if not...she'd give him a bucket—but she was *not* holding it for him this time. No way in hell. She was done holding puke buckets for him—his aim was off during his last come down, like he was gunning for her. She shuddered.

As they wound through the jungle, the path grew difficult to see; her night vision was good, but it wasn't spectacular. The brightest stars pierced the dusky sky, and trees appeared to meld together from the darkness. Twice, she stubbed her toe on some unseen obstacle. *Damn rocks just jump out at you sometimes,* she thought. Home wasn't far. They would arrive before sundown, avoiding most of the predators due to their nocturnal natures. She glanced back at Kotaris and noted he was more interested in his fingers than his environment; he wiggled his fingers and laughed.

What is he seeing?

Solaris grabbed the pink pendant hanging from her neck, the one her grandmother gave to her as a birthday gift and rubbed her thumb along the edge. Grandma explained it was a family heirloom but never bothered to mention why her mother didn't inherit it first, and...Solaris didn't care to ask. The truth was she liked it: the elegance of the metal incasing the crystal within, the characters inscribed down the side, and the way it came to a dagger point. Most of all, the piece reminded her of her grandma, and anything connected to her grandma was a good thing.

Solaris began to hum a song her grandma always sang to them as children. Even though she was completely unware she was humming, the act triggered a memory of a lecture from the old lady. *You remember what I told you child. It's your heritage as an Urokos, you know. The magic that runs through your veins is because you're tree kind, and we are strong!* She had said this while shaking her fist in the air and baring her teeth. As a young girl, it made her giggle, but with age came the realization that the old woman was serious.

"Granny?" asked Kotaris, causing her to snap out of the memory and stop humming.

"Yeah. It's grandma's song, Ko," she said as she slipped the necklace back under her shirt. She smiled at her brother, thinking how he often insisted on hearing the tune before he went to bed. Which was fine, of course.

Ka-boom!

The sound frightened her down to the ground, and she pulled Kotaris down beside her. The eruption was loud, and the shock wave vibrated the ground beneath their feet. All around them she could hear hundreds of birds taking flight. To top it all off, Kotaris was chiming in just in case she hadn't heard the noise.

"Boom-boom-boom-boo—"

"Kotaris, quiet," she said. He kept chanting. She wrapped her hands around his shoulders, giving him a quick shake. "I'm not playing. Be quiet and stay here. I'm serious, Ko."

Solaris realized she was pointing her finger at him; her parents pointed at him a lot, and she hated it. Solaris pulled her admonishing finger away and ran her hand through his hair instead.

"Go. Ko stay," he said. Then he fell to the ground with a defeated sigh, legs crossed, and hands resting in his lap.

She kissed him on his forehead. "Good, I'll be back real fast. Don't say anything and stay hidden."

Solaris began jogging toward the house when Kotaris shouted, "Careful…metal bird close. Careful."

CHAPTER 2

D avuk sat in the study of his summer cot-
tage. He looked up from the thick stack
of papers he read, took his glasses off, and
rubbed his temples. When he was satisfied the
massage wouldn't make his headache go away, he
set the contract down on his desk and stood up.
Davuk walked over to his window and looked out
into the jungle. Just beyond their family vehicle
was the one road into and out of their small plot
of land in the middle of nowhere. Any minute
now, Solaris and Kotaris should—had better come
marching through the front door.

He glanced over at the time display on
his desk and then back out of the window. They
should have been home thirty minutes prior, but
they were late. *Typical. Always pushing the limits.*
He would never tell them it was okay, but secretly,
he appreciated their small defiance as it would
carry them far in life, and he also understood the
joys of the wild. Davuk hadn't grown up in the jun-

gle as his wife Moranda had, but he loved it just as much, if not more than her. Maybe he had more love for it because he had grown up in Unikai. It had been a sprawling city then, but nothing compared to what it was now. So much had changed since the arrival of the first humans two decades before.

As a people, they were already spacefaring, but just to their own moon and not far beyond. Before the arrival of the aliens, there just hadn't been much interest in exploring space. Hell, at least half of Grea remained unexplored. The vast majority of the surface was covered by desert, except near the equator where the jungle and the river had a will of their own. Settlements flourished or vanished based on the whims of temperamental seasons, beasts, and local fauna. Whole areas of their world were simply left to the animals, plants, or the wind because it was too difficult to dominate the will of Green Mother.

The humans thought differently. Davuk turned from the window and picked up the contract again. On the front were four names and four lines. Three of them had signatures, except for the line next to his name. He had spent the better part of a year trying to convince himself that signing the contract was the right thing to do. The humans could then come in with their superior technology and help them subdue the rest of their planet...for a few very specific rights. He tossed the stack of papers back on the desk and then made his way out of the room.

He knew damn well the deal was lopsided. If someone was trying to get something from you, it was because they knew something you didn't. Whatever they were after had more perceived value than what they had to offer. They could just barter with knowledge or trade. Sure, it would take longer, but in the long run, they would catch up to the aliens and still own their planet. He wasn't going to be the asshole who sold his world to the edioka—the outsiders...the humans.

Davuk walked through his house looking for his wife. She wasn't in any of the rooms, so he made his way to the back porch and found her leaning against a post looking out over the back-yard. The yard wasn't remarkable other than grass needing to be cut, a babbling creek, and their marriage totem. It wasn't the best marriage totem, just the best they could afford at the time. *I'll need to hire someone to give a touch up*, he thought. The wood was aging and weathered, but it had held up well over the past twenty years. The names comprising the lines of their families were still legible...mostly. Times had become better; he might just go ahead and replace it.

Davuk pressed himself against his wife, slipped his arms around her waist, and kissed her on the neck. She moved her head towards him and moaned slightly.

"Hello, love," she said.

"Good evening, tree lady." He always called her tree lady given she was Urokos. It was his subtle joke about her having grown up in the less civilized regions of Grea.

"Ah," she said and turned, slipping her arms over his shoulders. "Mr. Provincer. I was just thinking we could sneak off to our room, but your statement made me realize you're much too sophisticated to be interested in anything as primal as what I had in mind. I'm sure you'd much rather be staring at some document or deciding how best to spend the city's construction budget."

"Moranda," he said turning his nose up. "At this time of the day? What kind of man do you take me for?"

"The kind who likes to please his wife?"

He pulled her close, running his hand through the back of her hair, and—then the votech rang. It was coming from his office. They both placed their foreheads together, chuckled, and then Davuk gave her a quick kiss on the lips. "I'll be right back, and we can continue this discussion about how much I please my wife."

She smiled with raised eyebrows and gave a little wave.

Davuk jogged back into the house and found his votech lying on the couch of his study

—one of the kids must have been playing with it as he never left it there. He tapped the screen and said, "Accept."

"Afternoon, Davuk. Do you have a moment?" asked Rokum. Rokum was one of the four people selected to review and sign the agreement currently sitting on his desk. He also happened to have a large opportunity that would become open to him if the deal went through; an opportunity he had not yet disclosed to the Council on Alien Affairs.

"Yeah, Rokum. I'm here, what do you need?" asked Davuk.

"Did you get a chance to review the document?"

"Yes."

"And?"

"I just don't think it's in our best interest to sign this."

"Davuk...why?"

"Why? Why would we give them such generous land rights? A one-hundred-year lease in a prime location with complete legal jurisdiction just seems one-sided with no upfront payment or trade."

"It's about progress, Davuk. How many times do I have to tell you that? If they put down roots here, then their technology and knowledge will proliferate into our own through assimilation."

"Assimilation, huh?"

"Yes! Besides, what right do we have to their technology before we offer them something worth their while. All they see now are a bunch of fucking wild people running around—half of them are barely clothed and still using spears, for Green Mother's sake! They could give us god damned clothes to give out, and it would be a fair trade as far as I'm concerned."

"Rokum, in two decades, what have we really learned or gotten from them?"

"A lot. Look at how well our communication networks have improved."

"You mean those of us who aren't running around with spears are now running around with our faces glued to some machine watching images move? Using the satellites they provided, by-the-way. We didn't put them there, and we still haven't been allowed access to any of the designs. How convenient almost all of our communications are now going through machinery they control."

"Well…"

"I can think of better examples, so let me help you. How about loss of cultural identity, tension buildup between the Urokos and Provincers, and gonorrhea. Those three things have impacted us the most since their arrival."

"You can't hold that against them, Davuk."

"The hell I can't! The first thing they did was come down here and tell us how backward everything we do is, and then they accidently spread a disease killing three thousand of our own before we got it under control. Notice I said we. Meanwhile, they are up there asking us for food and water. Who do you think's going to end up supporting them? Look...I'm not saying that I'm entirely against them, or that good can't come from collaboration. We just don't need to treat them like our superiors as it sends the wrong message. They aren't that different from us, other than a few fancier guns and ships. We need to look out for ourselves first and when a real option gets put on the table where both of our peoples can get mutual benefit, I'll sign the line."

"Davuk, all progress requires sacrifice. We risk a little now for much greater rewards later. You know this."

"I won't sign it, Rokum."

"I think you need to reconsider, Davuk. Think hard about your position and where you would like to be. Men who stand in the way of progress often find themselves removed."

"Are you threatening me?"

"I'm telling you to get your idealistic ass out of the way and let our people partner with the humans."

"Progress...how about I tell the council how much you'll benefit from this deal?"

"What?"

"I know about the deal you made with them ,Rokum, but I've chosen not to think about it too much or speak up about it. If you keep threatening me, I'll make sure everyone is aware of your waiting financial windfall."

"Brokering deals is not against the law, Davuk."

"Secret collusion against your own people is immoral, Rokum. If it's so innocent then why haven't you made it more apparent that you own the option on the land you are pushing for us to give them? How many hands did you have to fill to keep that from coming out during the land hearing?"

"We're all entitled to our privacy, and I don't have to explain myself to you or anyone else. In fact, what you're saying right now reinforces why I'm doing it. You're just a speciest! You think them less than us, simply because they are not us."

"I think less of them because they do backroom deals with weak fah'dienh and abduct our women to sell in secret!"

"I can't believe you are falling for that propaganda! It's just stories the Urokos spread to drive a wedge between us and them, but I see where you stand. I can't convince you to change your mind then?"

"Jump a cliff, Rokum."

"I was hoping to send someone out to pick up the contract from you, Davuk, but I see that isn't going to happen."

"Your intuition is just astounding."

"I'll let him know the plans have changed Davuk. Goodbye."

Davuk turned off the votech, flung it at the couch, and ran his fingers through his hair. He closed his eyes and then opened them again when he heard the floor creek. Moranda was standing in the doorway with a smirk.

"I see you're trying to become friends with Rokum."

"I told him to go jump a cliff."

"Yeah, I heard. Not very professional of you."

"Well," he said, holding his hands up.

"It's okay, love. I actually didn't come in to ride you about your diplomatic skills. I remembered, we need to talk about Solaris and specifically the key."

Davuk sat down in his chair and leaned over, resting his elbows on his knees. "Yeah, her birthday is in a couple months, isn't it? I guess it's time she be let in on the Bokatari Covenant. Especially, since your mother gave her that damn key already? Why would she do that before Solaris has been sworn in?"

Moranda shrugged. "Select few actually know what it is, and even fewer know how to use it. The only ones that do are the Hadagii Elken, and they are coming to talk to her tomorrow—not in a couple months."

"What?"

"It's like a pre-meeting so she won't be so shocked when she participates in the revealing."

"I never got a pre-meeting."

"You were never responsible for a gate key. A special one at that."

"Do you really believe what they say about it?"

"You mean do I think it's really a key to Armatoran?"

"No. I mean, do you think it's alive? If it is, do you think Solaris should really have that responsibility? She's only seen seventeen springs. That's a hell of a burden, don't you think?"

"Where was all this when mother first bestowed it to her years ago?"

Davuk stood up and put his hands in his pockets. "Well...I guess it didn't seem so important then. She was my little girl and really didn't know everything else. She's going to be exposed to everything now, Moranda. What if she's not ready? What if she doesn't believe or worse? If she goes too far?"

Moranda laughed. "Oh, she'll believe when a Hadagii Elken takes her through a gate for her pilgrimage."

"Green Mother! She has to go to Armatoran? You never told me that, Moranda. No. Absolutely not! That place is death trap! I will not allow this!"

"Davuk. What did you think was going to happen?" she asked and walked over to her husband. His hands were out of his pockets and placed on his hips. Moranda put her arms around her husband's waist and hugged him, rested her head on his chest. "She is a key guardian. By the end of this, she will know more than we do, love."

"Moranda. Armatoran is dangerous; she could die there!"

"She could die here."

"It's not the same!"

"I'm sure Otro will be taking her on the pilgrimage. He is one of the most prominent modern Hadagii Elken to date. He has led many to Armatoran, countless times, and brought them back unscathed. She'll be fine. I'm more worried about poor Kotaris. He won't know what to do without her."

"Ko will be fine. I'm not worried about him. I want to meet Otro before she goes."

"Of course, love. And now," she said, while walking her fingers up his chest and smiling. "You're so tense. I think you need to stop focusing on all these other issues and focus on me. You were telling me earlier about how much you love pleasing me?"

"Do you hear that?"

"What?'" she asked and then kissed his neck.

"No, wait, Moranda. Do you hear that? It sounds like there is a shuttle nearby."

CHAPTER 3

The captain sat on a crate in the cargo hold. He had one leg hiked up onto a small ammunition box and a half-finished bottle of synthetic whiskey in his free hand. No one aboard knew his real name, and that was how he kept it. To them, he was only the captain. From time-to-time, he would find himself pondering whether he could be construed as a mercenary or a pirate captain. Did the jobs he accepted dictate his status or his intentions? Did the fact he accepted jobs automatically put him into mercenary classification? In his mind, pirates were always after treasure and their actions never held any significant position for the greater good. Mercenaries, however, could seek fortune and fight for a cause. Whether the cause was just or not was ultimately up to the eye of the beholder. In his experience, both sides were usually full of shit and comprised of assholes just waiting for an opportunity to take advantage of some other man's weak position. Life was a bitch.

Most of the time, he was less romantic and simply fancied himself a pioneer of aggressive interstellar diplomatic relations, smuggling, and pillaging.

He leaned over, grabbing a dangling latch chain to balance himself so he could get a better position. Damn bulky armor made moving difficult at times. He needed to invest in a full powered armor suit. Just as tough, but not as cumbersome. Currently, the only thing powered on his suit was the arms.

He leaned forward, bringing the flaming wreckage into view. Less than a dozen meters away, blue flames leapt from a contorted mass of metal. It had once been a vehicle. As he stared at the wreck, he felt a pang of regret that they hadn't searched the vehicle before destroying it. *Could have been something valuable in there.* He smiled. *Definitely a pirate. A space pirate. Ha!*

The smoldering mass was the problem with last minute operations...insufficient planning. Give a bunch of hot-heads guns, and they start blowing shit up. Go figure. He sighed and used the chain to pull himself up to his feet. He steadied himself, turned up the bottle and pounded down the rest of the liquor. He held the bottle into the air and shook it until the last drop fell into his open mouth, groaned and then flung the empty bottle through the open cargo bay.

The man turned on his heels to face into the belly of his jumper. His contracted reconnaissance technician was swiping madly across the display visual and muttering under his breath. He couldn't remember the man's name. What he did remember was wanting to throw the asshole out of the airlock several times because he was an incompetent puke. He narrowed his eyes at the man, trying to remember why he hadn't thrown him out but couldn't. *Oh well*, he thought. *There's always the return trip.*

"Tell me what I can't see," he said.

The technician leaned over the panel and then cut his hand through the image, causing it to distort and shimmer. "Fuck," he shouted. "I hate this fucking planet!" He either wasn't paying attention or was outright ignoring the captain. Neither was acceptable.

The captain reached down into a toolbox, pulled out a bolt and hurled it at the man. The piece of metal struck the technician across the forehead. The brigand recoiled against the wall and dropped his hand down onto his pistol, but as his scowling eyes fell upon the captain's visage, they immediately cut away; he snatched his hand from the butt of his pistol and straightened his back.

"Now that I have your attention, tell me what you see."

The man dropped back down onto stiffened arms, leaning over the hovering images. He took a deep breath and then coughed. "It's not clear. Well, it was... but now it's clear as a shit storm. I've tried to filter the noise out, but there's something penetrating our tech shields."

"Can you triangulate the source of the interference?"

"No. It's coming from everywhere. I'm guessing, but I think it's just the damn planet. Some material we've never seen before. Maybe those pink crystals. There seems to be a larger concentration of them in this area, and this is where we are having the most trouble. I don't know what else to tell you. The feed has been coming and going, but now it's just...gone."

"I see. Were you able to make out anything before it began malfunctioning?"

"Not much. Even before it quit altogether, the output was jacked, but...something did come across. Didn't seem important."

"I decide what's important. Explain...*not much*," said the captain.

The man straightened again and brought his hand under his chin. "A cluster of movement heading in our direction from the west...about ten miles out, but there's nothing out that way except jungle."

"West. You mean it's in line with that tree village we hit?"

The technician looked down and then back up. "Yeah, now that you mention it. I guess so."

"And you don't think that's fucking important?"

The man swallowed.

The captain rubbed his temples. "Any idea what it was? Can you tell how many?" he asked, unclipping the tether holding his pistol in place as he walked back to the man. He made his way around the side of the panels so he could stand face to face with the technician.

The man was quiet until the captain's hand slipped away from the pistol. Then he shook his head. "No telling. Nearest settlement from here is that one roughly twenty miles west. I don't think those tree huggers could have covered ground that fast Captain. I think it might just be animals."

"Coming this way, after the explosion?"

"Uh..yeah. I guess so."

The captain slammed his palm against the man's head and drove it into the control panel. He pressed down until he heard the technician gasp in pain. "Animals don't move toward explosions," he shouted. "I want the panel operational now. I'm paying you a lot of money to watch our asses. Fix it," he screamed. "Or I'll fix you."

On his way out of the craft, the captain ran his fingers along the cages, watching the females cower into their corners as he passed. The red cargo lamp was on, and it made the women look as if they had a light red tint to their skin. All eyes diverted from him as he made his way. He stopped to tap his fingers on the last empty cage and then turned to look at the faces of his newest stock. All in all, they weren't a bad catch; most were middle aged, but the majority of them were pretty, and beauty could make up for some of the aging. However, one or two were average at best. He considered releasing them but decided against it. Two in the hand is better than one in the bush. Besides, some depraved bastard would be into it anyway. Some men didn't appreciate their women to be better looking than themselves, even when they bought them. *Still,* he thought. *One young one would be worth more than this entire lot.*

The captain sold his bounty in lots. Discretion was key, and selling in bulk to a middleman was the best way to do it. Fewer transactions. A little less profit but a lot less exposure risk. Technically, his actions weren't illegal yet, but he saw no point in drawing unnecessary attention to himself or the Vitor. Overzealous human rights activists were always looking for any just cause. *Or would they be an alien activist? Doesn't fucking matter.* He twisted his mouth and brought his dark eyes upon the closest female. Her eyes met his for a brief moment and then she turned from him to rest her head against the back of the cage.

Her movement caused a dry tear track to glimmer across a bruised cheek. *I need to remind the men to go easier on the females.* It was strange to look at the creatures and see so many human features, even though their species were separated by such great distances.

The captain marched down the ramp and studied his surroundings. To his pleasure, the largest portion of his men had set up a perimeter around the operations. Good execution. At least they did that right. The wood and concrete dwelling was centered in a clearing with only one road in and out. Surrounding them was the rapidly darkening jungle on all sides. These beings hadn't conquered their environment yet. Grea held secrets in wait for the right men to come along and claim them. He thought about the cluster of movement heading in their direction and rubbed his forehead. The captain raked his hand across his brow and slung the sweat to the ground. *We need to hurry.*

He suspected the extraction team was already inside the dwelling pursuing their objective as he walked toward the house, and then he knew they were, as a hysterical feminine voice erupted from inside. After the shriek came a sharp crash, aggressive shouting, and then silence. The captain waited by the entrance, studying the surroundings until his earpiece roared to life. "Pfzzt… There's another bitch with the target—," said the voice before being cut off. One of the mercenaries yelled as wood splintered over something hard. "The target is putting up a helluva fight. A lot more than the last asshole."

The captain stopped and pressed his fingers to his throat, "Acknowledged. How old is she?"

"She's a little older, Captain."

Fuck. Where are all the young females on this planet?

The captain paused, before responding.

"Captain?"

"Yeah," he said and chewed his bottom lip. "Bring the male out. Leave the woman inside."

"You want us to let the female go?"

"No. I want you to bring the target out and hold on to the fucking woman until I tell you different."

"On our way," came the voice.

Two men were standing guard at the entrance of the house; the captain pointed at the one on the right and gestured for him to scout the perimeter. The man nodded and jogged away toward the edge of the clearing. Within seconds, he disappeared into the trees. The captain returned his attention to the dwelling. The door was hanging ajar, giving a clear view of a desperate struggle. The mercenary in front was pulling the target by a neck snare, and the one behind was pushing him; using the pole as a prodding device. The target thrashed to get free but couldn't do much as his hands were bound behind his back. To his credit, he fought the entire way, but they managed to bring him out.

The male was a large one for their species, broad chested and tall. When he was free of the building, his captors assumed a position on both sides of him and tightened down on their neck snares. The wires bit into the target's already bleeding neck until he collapsed onto the ground. The captain watched as the being gasped and coughed; watched the veins bulge up its neck and across its tan forehead. The captain held up his hand for the men to ease off. They nodded, loosened their respective snares, and the target jerked his head up, gasping for air.

The captain took a knee in front of the being, put a gloved finger under his chin, and then forced him to look up. "Do you love your woman?"

The being stared at the captain for a moment and then looked away in response.

"You know...this is only going to go my way," said the captain as he cracked his knuckles and stood up. "Right now, I'm indifferent about *your* woman. I just want what I came for, and believe it or not, that's a good place for you and your cuddle buddy to be. Now, do you love your woman or not?"

The being looked up at the captain and growled something before baring its teeth.

In response, the captain dug his armored index finger into the side of the target's cheek and then plopped his hand on top of the being's head. He turned the target's head left and then right before violently pushing it away. The captain pressed his fingers to his own throat, "Bill, you and your boys go inside and find their laundry room. Bring out the clothes and dump them at the ramp."

"Pzzzt...Okay," responded several of his men. He watched as men left their posts and jogged toward the house. After watching them disappear into the dwelling, the captain turned toward the kneeling being. He plopped his heavy hand on top of the thing's head and ruffled its hair before slipping the nooses off its neck.

"It's my understanding that your women are anatomically close to my people's women. Little longer in the ears, and hair is a little different but the same everywhere else it counts. And no babies...*yet,* but isn't it amazing that were hundreds of light years apart, and somehow I can bump uglies with your woman? Isn't that some shit? Not only that, but I understand that there is something about your species' particular physiology that heightens the sexual pleasure for humans. It's like...like something planned all this. Fate or some god...or some jungle bitch? Isn't that what your people believe in? Regardless, it brought us here...brought me here to you...right now."

The being stared at the captain, its eyes narrowed and nostrils flared. It followed the captain as he paced back and forth.

"So wild, that men are willing to pay me a lot of money to bring their pretty little asses back into orbit. I hear making love to fah'dienh is like a drug, and these fuckers are willing to start a war over it to get them. And since I'm being honest, I want you to know that I've been professional. As a general rule, I haven't sampled my product, but......now I'm getting curious. What do you think about us looking into this together?" asked the captain as he bent down next to Davuk's ear. "How about I have my way with your woman right here in front of you? See what the fuss is all about?"

The hostage roared a string of alien words he couldn't understand, and the captain pulled back, nodding with mock approval. The tone was definitely hostile and would need to change. He eyed the being, tightened his armored hand into a fist until it was rock solid. He kept his eyes locked with Davuk's as he slowly wound his body to the right, readying it to be released in one explosive movement. He waited, searching for the right moment. The wind gently caressed them, lapping at their skin as the failing light sharpened the shadows on their faces. And then she screamed. Davuk's eyes widened, and he tried to look beyond the captain to find his wife.

Now!

The captain slammed his armored knuckles into Davuk's cheek, ripped the skin and sent violet blood bursting into the air. The alien lurched to the left from the impact, took in a deep, shaky breath and then brought himself back upright to lock eyes with the captain. The right side of his face was already swelling, closing his eye shut. Davuk sucked in a sharp breath through clenched teeth, doing his best to stay upright and process what just happened. The captain could see he was struggling to stay conscious, much less upright. The force from his mechanically enhanced arms probably wasn't much less than what someone could deliver with a bat. Of course, he pulled the punch—a little.

The captain turned Davuk's head so he could see the wound. *Damn, I hit him too hard. He doesn't have much time.* "Let's cut the shit, Davuk. I know you understand me. I've swung by your lovely home on business to see you off. Some of your enlightened brethren have asked for you to be removed from the picture. Something about stalling diplomatic relations, but we both know that's just code for, you're costing someone money. You should have just signed the goddamn trade agreement. And now, I've been brought into the situation, and your wife is here…," he said and let the being's head go. "Pay attention, Davuk. Quit looking at the woods. You're on my list, and there is only one way off my list. Give me what I want, and I won't throw your wife in a cage."

"What do you want?" he asked in the trade language.

"Ah. You see," said the captain. "I knew we could come to terms. Back to my original question. Do you love your woman?"

"Yes," Davuk said and closed his eyes.

"Wonderful! I'm glad that you do. So, here's my proposition. I will let your woman go if I can find a suitable replacement. I've got enough old ones. You tell me where I can find a nice-looking young lady. She doesn't have to be beautiful, just younger. After I find said lady, I will let your woman go and put your selection in her place. Obviously, if you lie, and I don't find a good replacement, I will just have to keep her. Now, I think that's quite the bargain. Don't you?" he asked. The captain straightened a little and opened his hand in diplomacy. "And I am a lot of things, but a liar is not one of them. Hard to get people to trust you with contracts if they think you are a liar. Know what I mean?"

Davuk didn't say anything. The being

looked at the captain, then toward the woods, and then back toward the dwelling.

"I cannot do that to my own people," he said and closed his eyes.

"I see," said the captain. He pressed his fingers to his throat, "Bring the woman out."

The captain watched the entrance patiently and then smiled when he saw the female emerge from its dark interior. She was a beautiful creature and unmarred. The cushioned neck ties were working as planned. He couldn't see a single bruise around her thin neck. He made a mental note that he needed to buy more of them. After the men reached their position, they forced her to her knees and the captain marched over to her.

"Please," said Davuk. "Let her go! Don't do this!"

The female looked wildly from the captain and then to her mate. She started shouting something the captain couldn't understand and began crying. Davuk responded to her with a reassuring tone; however, he only managed to say a few words before his voice cracked from emotion. The captain reached the woman and then gently patted her head as she sobbed. Through sobs, she said something to Davuk, and the male immediately started shouting at her with wide eyes. The captain paused to let this image sink in, and then he grabbed a handful of her hair and jerked her head back and forth. She cried out with a shrill scream until she was out of breath and then settled into a sob.

"Please stop," cried out Davuk.

"I'm waiting. Tell me where to go," the captain said and smiled.

"I...I...," he said then began speaking rapidly to the woman in his native language. Just as quickly, she responded between sobs.

"You really just refuse to accept her situation, don't you?" asked the captain. He left one hand firmly rooted in her hair and ripped the female's shirt from her body with the other. She screamed and tried to jerk away, but the captain's grip was vice-like in her long dark hair. He gave a quick jolt, straightening her upright so Davuk could see her well.

"You see her?" he asked and then threw her to the ground. "This will be her life until she dies!" The captain planted a heavy boot on her back and pressed her chest into the ground. He motioned for the men to remove their snares, and they did so. She wailed and sobbed on the ground as the captain ground his boot into her back and stared at Davuk. He slipped one of his hands from his side and brought it up to his belt buckle and ran his index finger back and forth over the metal prong.

Davuk lunged forward to shoulder ram the captain, but the mercenary to the right with—a practiced precision—looped the snare around the being's neck and slung him to the ground. Suddenly, he roared and rose to his feet, overpowering the man with the snare to the point that the second mercenary had to step in. The second man rammed the blunt end of the snare into the creature's sternum and dropped him to his knees. He then tossed the snare to the side, pulled a slide stick free and snapped it down so it was fully extended. He raised the stick into the air and then paused long enough to look at the captain. The captain nodded, and the man brought down the weapon upon the alien. Davuk tried many different actions to escape or thwart the beating, but it only served to make his captors laugh and lash out harder. Finally, the second man kicked him in the ribs and then backed away.

"Spirited, isn't he?" asked the captain. The other men laughed and nodded in agreement as Davuk slid his face across the dirt to look towards his wife. He mumbled several words and then a strange noise came from him. He turned from her and drove his face into the ground.

"Captain," said the mercenary to his left.

"What?"

"Sir. The woman…"

The captain looked down at the woman and noticed she was motionless. Dark blood pooled around her head. "What the fuck?" he shouted as he quickly pulled his boot from her back. He stared at her motionless body for several seconds before he gripped her shoulder and pulled her over. The woman was gurgling and coughing up blood, staring up into the darkening sky. She blinked twice and then he saw and felt her life leave her body. Blood covered the lower half of her face and oozed from a hole in her throat. The captain watched as the blood stopped and then examined a sharp root protruding from the ground. It didn't take him long to realize he had impaled her on the root. The captain let her fall out of his arms, and then he stood over her body for a moment, analyzing what had happened.

"Go prep the shuttle for launch."

The men looked at each other and then down at Davuk.

"Now!"

The men nodded and jogged toward the craft.

"Alright, Davuk," said the captain as he made his way over to the man. "The deal has changed, but I still want a girl. You get to decide whether I kill you quick or take my time. We're going to load up in my craft, and I'm going to start cutting parts off of you every hour until my last cage has a woman in it. And don't worry. I have a medic, and even though he doesn't know shit about fah'dienh medicine, I'm guessing cauterizing works for you guys too. So...quick or slow?"

Davuk groaned and then brought himself up onto his knees. He looked up at the captain as a flash of lightning ran across the sky. The being turned its head skyward as drops of rain began to come down. It held its face upturned for a moment then brought it back down to lock eyes with the captain.

"As you humans say, go fuck yourself."

The captain slammed his knuckles into Davuk's face again, toppling him to the ground. He paused for a moment and then hammer fisted the man. "Where?" he shouted. Again, he brought down another hammer fist. "Where?" A third hammer fist. "Where, goddamn it?" He drew his arm back to strike again, waiting for a response, but Davuk gave none. He grabbed him by his hair and drug him through the yard toward the burning vehicle. Although it had begun raining, it wasn't heavy enough to extinguish the flames. Once they were mere yards from the flaming mass, he released Davuk's hair and then brought the heel of his boot down on his knee. The creature's bone snapped, and the alien doubled over, holding its leg and screaming. The captain let him writhe on the ground for several seconds before he squatted down beside him.

"I'm a fucking pirate, Davuk. You get it? No planet! No mercy! No fucks given! Give me what

I want, and there will be no more pain. No more worry. Look where you are. No one's coming for you. *Where* is a girl?" he demanded and jerked Davuk up by his ponytail. Blood and saliva dangled from his mouth. Davuk swallowed and closed his eyes but only for a moment. Then he looked up at the captain and spat in his face. "I'm a Green. We bow to no one."

The captain pulled on Davuk's hair until he grunted and then snatched his head to the side before releasing him. *Fuck.* He looked around at the dark jungle and then down at Davuk. The being wouldn't talk. He knew it now, as sure as he was standing there. No matter what he did, this thing would refuse to tell him anything. He glanced at the fire and pondered if burning the being would make it talk, and then he remembered the mass of movement on the tracking panel; it was heading right for them. Whatever it was would be on top of them soon.

The captain grabbed the man by the back of his neck and his belt loop and threw him against the burning vehicle. Davuk screamed as the fire took hold of his clothes and rolled away from the searing hulk of metal. Before he could squirm far, the captain secured his hand into the back of the being's hair and then brought the man's face close to the flaming wreck.

Davuk pleaded in his native language. The captain wasn't exactly sure what the creature was saying, but he felt confident he grasped the meaning. Please don't. Something along those lines. "Where?" he shouted.

Again, the being was repeating what it said before. As the captain listened he realized Davuk wasn't pleading with him. He recognized the same pattern in human men.

"Are you fucking praying?" he shouted and then pressed Davuk's face to the hot metal. "Nobody is coming to save you!" Davuk screamed as his face sizzled against the flaming wreck until the captain snatched him away. He watched as the man squirmed on the ground and rolled in agony across the grass.

"Never," repeated the man before he began to speak in his native language again.

The captain stood over Davuk and then glanced at the darkening woods again. He sighed. "I believe you," said the captain as he unfastened his pistol. He held the gun against the target's head as he mumbled. Davuk was shaking as the words left bloody, trembling lips. The captain wondered if it was fear or rage gripping Davuk in his last moment. Maybe both? He waited until Davuk finished a cycle of the repetitions and then he pulled the trigger. The side of Davuk's head exploded and expelled its contents across the yard. The man slumped to the ground and moved no more.

"We're done," he whispered.

The captain stared at the corpse and felt a twinge of respect for the corpse formerly known as Davuk. He holstered his pistol and then turned as he heard someone coming up from behind him.

"Captain," said the man.

The captain brushed past him. "You better have a damn good reason for leaving your post, son."

"Sir, it's the clothes pile. I think there may be another female."

CHAPTER 4

She jumped as the sound ambushed her. Solaris sank to her knees and pressed hard against her ears. She rested her head against the tree trunk wishing she were deaf. She wanted to run or fight, anything but freeze, but her legs wouldn't move. She shook violently and dug her nails into her head. *What would they want me to do?* Their main concern would have been her and her brother's safety. She could hear her parents say, *Get your brother and go to Grandma's. We love you.* She could almost feel them hug her as she heard their voices in her head. She needed to vomit and then she coughed. The cough quickly slipped into a sob and then she slapped her hand over her mouth. She was the only one left to help take care of him. It was just so hopeless; she knew of only one choice.

Suddenly, an arm snagged around her waist and another slapped across her mouth. She tried to let out a cry, but the hand muffled the sound.

The man snatched her away from the tree, pulling her from her feet. She struggled to get free, but her captor was too strong and began dragging her away as she kicked and writhed. She could feel the reeking hot breath on her neck. The man slipped his arm up and began to fondle her breast and then he pulled some device from his belt. With what appeared to be well seasoned movements, he shoved the contraption into her mouth which secured itself to her head. The straps of the device tightened down, choking out any of her cries.

"Yeah, bitch. I think I'll have some fun with you first," he whispered and tugged at her pants, but they held fast. Solaris screamed, but only a muffled sound escaped.

"No reason all the richies get to have you to their selves. It's you and me first, and then I'll take you back on—"

She felt the panic swelling in her chest as his breath assaulted the side of her neck, and then he was jerked away with a resounding *crack*. The hands restraining her simply fell away as she crawled out from underneath the man. She heard the body collapse on the ground and spun to see what had happened.

The human was crumpled over with his head facing in the wrong direction. Her brother stood over the man, pointing at him and then he said one word, "No." After his statement he looked up, first at Solaris, and then past her, to their parents lying on the ground. "Mommy...Da?"

He started forward, but Solaris wrapped her arms around him and held as firmly as she could. She felt so safe pressed against him, her giant guardian. She didn't want him to run out there and get killed. She knew she couldn't contain him, but she had to try; she just couldn't survive losing anymore family. *Stay! Please gods stay. You have to understand!*

Solaris wanted to scream, fight, cry, anything besides sit there. She could still feel the human's hand on her bosom; it made her feel dirty. Despite her own raging feelings, she tried to console her brother by patting him on the head as some kind of assurance all would be well. It usually worked, and it was the only thing she could think of at the time, but limited as his intelligence was, he understood death. And Mommy and Da were gone forever.

She looked up at him; both his eyes were agape, and she could see fresh tears streaming from the corners. His lips trembled. He tried to mumble something, but she shook her head and pulled him tighter into her arms. He hugged her back, letting out a series of small sobs, burying his face into her neck. She brought both of them down beside a tree, wiped away her own tears and then his. Solaris pulled at the device on her face, but it wouldn't come loose. She looked at the man on the ground. If a key existed to unlock the mechanical gag, then it could be on his body, but she wouldn't even know what it looked like if she found it. Instead, she picked her tattered shirt of the ground and tied it around her upper body.

Solaris grabbed Kotaris by his head and pointed into the woods shaking her head *yes.*

"No," he cried, snot running off his chin. "Dead...dead. Mommy! Da," he cried, as he stretched his arm out toward their fallen parents' bodies, fingers rapidly slicing through the air.

Solaris covered his mouth with one hand and gave a quiet gesture to her own mouth with the other. He seemed to understand, but then he crawled over to the dead man and pushed him around creating an alarming rustling noise in the leaves. Before she could do anything, he yanked hard on the man's belt flipping the corpse into the air. Kotaris shuffled back to his sister—a knife in hand. Of course, she thought as she took the knife from him and cut the straps to the device around her head. She hugged her brother and wiped another tear from her cheek. Solaris took his hand in hers and turned to leave but then paused. *What if there were more men out there? Waiting,* she thought and looked down at the human on the ground. *Like that one? Or maybe he was the only one. But even if more were prowling around, there are worse things in the jungle.* Solaris sucked in her breath, preventing herself from releasing another sob. The jungle was far from safe at night. It might even be less safe than cowering near a group of murderers. *What do I do? Shit, okay…when you can't make a good decision it's because you need more information. So…*

"I need to get a little closer, Ko. I have to hear what they are saying." She couldn't believe what she was saying, but she had to know if the ambusher was just a chance encounter or if they were coming after them. *I have to take care of my brother now,* she thought. *I have to take care of myself. I have to be strong.*

"No," he cried again. "Kill-kill-kill-kill."

"Ko," she said and brought his forehead to her own. "I have to. Do you trust me?"

"Mmm."

"Do you trust me?"

"Yah," he managed between sobs.

"I know you don't understand, but I have to go down there to see what they are doing. If I can't, then I can't help us survive. You want to live, right?"

"Yah," he pleaded.

"Then let me go. Just for a moment."

"Mmm," he protested, but he let her slip away and turned onto his side, curling into a ball.

Solaris belly crawled toward the tree line again to get to where she could hear the men better. She needed to know what their plans were, or where they were going. Hopefully, they would give something away. If they were going to give chase, then it was to the caves of the summit with her and Kotaris, but if they weren't, she wanted to stay put. Someone would come for them if they just stayed put. After getting into position, she could see them more clearly because the sun had set, and the ship's flood lights were on. There were nine men circled around the edge of the drop hatch to the space craft, all armored and all armed. The man who she assumed was the leader stood on the ramp of the craft and motioned as he talked; a pair of her pants were on his shoulder. She pricked up her ears to better hear their conversation but couldn't make out much of what was said because of the distance. Her father had paid for lessons on the human trade language after school and she found it ironic those lessons might actually save her life now.

She watched the leader as he stayed on the ramp; he gazed calmly, scanning the woods and then he stopped in her direction. Solaris froze on the spot, even holding her breath. The man seemed to be staring right at her, as if he could see her. It was like he was saying: *I know you're there.*

No…that's impossible, she thought, *He can't see me…can he?*

The man eventually looked over his shoulder and shouted, "Release the tracker." Then he dangled her pants to the side. *What is he doing? What's a tracker?* Something large enough to shake the craft came up behind him and began sniffing and prodding the pants. The creature belched some horrible squeal and continued down off the craft. *Oh, no.*

Solaris didn't care to see the tracker up close—it was time to leave. She raced back to her brother, who was fiddling with another of the dead man's weapons. She snagged his hand and pulled them deeper into the woods, and eventually, he pulled away and ran alongside her. Kotaris didn't resist, so she assumed he must understand they needed to leave. She was thankful, at least for that.

The siblings ripped through the jungle as fast as their legs could carry them. They followed the trail up to the second fork and then abruptly turned off the path until they reached the stream. Then they waded up the ankle-deep creek, heedless of the splashing noises it made; she figured it wouldn't matter, because the bugs were singing in full force for them, as if this night would be their last. When the stream dead ended into a waterfall, they veered to the left again, climbed a small bluff and continued up the slope on a second less obvious path.

Eventually, Solaris could take no more pain in her side. She finally brought herself down to a trot, then a walk, and at last, she stopped altogether. She hunched over in exhaustion for a moment and then straightened her back, filling her lungs with as much air as possible. Through her gasps, she managed to steal a glimpse of Kotaris—he stood motionless, one hand on a hip, the other still grasping the stick weapon he took from the dead human. One could barely even notice the flare of his nostrils or the rise of his chest. He wasn't winded at all.

She shook her head, wishing she had some of his endurance. *At least he looks calm. He seems to have forgotten about what just happened. Out of sight, out of mind, right? Or maybe…maybe I'm not giving him enough credit.* The image of him standing over the dead man entered her mind. *No*, he had commanded.

Kotaris turned and looked behind them and then jerked his attention back to Solaris. "We go," he said.

"I…I…need more time," she said, through gasps. *Damn. We must have already run three river spans. Give me a break, they can't be that close after all that.*

"No. Go now," he shouted, scooped her over his shoulder and started running again.

"Damnit, Ko, put me down. I can run," she shouted.

He answered with a grunt she recognized as *no*.

Crunch!

The sound came close behind them, and then it was followed by another and another. Solaris looked up watching the upper part of the trees; most just shook, but the smaller ones fell shortly after they passed by them. Then she was able to make out the loud grunts of the beast closing in about the time she noticed its outline—it was huge—and it was gaining. Then the beast saw them and squealed with excitement. Its eyes—they were glowing red.

"Never mind," she shouted. "Haul-ass!"

A loud explosion ripped overhead, and she knew the sound came from the humans' jumper. A succession of heavy thuds pounded the ground off to the right—brigands landing after leaping from the spacecraft. They were coming, and as they drew closer, she could hear their shouts. Short command bursts. They seemed to be concerned about the beast getting to Solaris before they could.

"To the left, Ko," said Solaris. Then it dawned on her. *We've pinned ourselves right next to the cliffs.*

Her brother veered so hard to the left, he nearly lost her, and she would have fallen, had he not grabbed her at the last minute. As he threw her back over his shoulder, she realized the vegetation had disappeared in front of them.

"Stop," she yelled.

Kotaris slammed on his brakes, and they slid to a hault only meters away from a hundred-foot drop. She jumped off his back and ran to the edge...it was too sheer to climb down. Kotaris looked at his sister, and she returned his look. She didn't know what else to do. Jump maybe. She looked down the cliff again, but she just couldn't. Then Kotaris, with gentle hands, reached for his sister and pulled her close to him.

"Kotaris protect Solaris."

"SQEEEEEEEEEEEEEEEEEEEEE."

The beast erupted from the brush and charged for the fah'dienh siblings. It was the size her father's car and looked like a mechanical nightmare from hell. Large curved tusks protruded from a long snout and its wide head was fitted with gleaming metal plates. A stiff black mane trailed down its neck and across a broad back down to stubby, hooved legs. The animal glared at them with hateful, red eyes and squealed again.

Kotaris pushed his sister away as the thing fell upon them. When it did, he threw his fist into the side of the creature's face, releasing a tremendous smack as he made contact. To her shock, the beast stumbled, but it quickly regained its composure and spun on its haunches, seizing Kotaris's forearm in its mouth. It jerked the young man off his feet and then power drove him into the ground, using its metal plated head as a battering ram.

Kotaris responded by pounding the creature with the stick weapon he had pulled off of the dead human. As the monster plowed him through the ground, he slapped the beast repeatedly with the stick. Suddenly, the momentum caused the black weapon to shoot outward, doubling in length, the tip ending in a sharp point.

By this time Solaris had risen to her feet. "Stab him, Ko! Stab him," she shouted.

The beast released its grip on the young man's arm and snatched him off the ground with one of its large tusks. Kotaris flew into the air until the force of gravity drove him downward, his mauled arm flapping helplessly.

As he came down, he drove the stake home into the creature's glowing eye. It was as if he had pressed a button. The cybernetic creature slapped Kotaris away with its bulky head and squealed horribly, trying to escape the blinding pain in its eye.

The giant staggered to the left first, and then shuffled far to the right, shaking its head violently. The overcorrection caused it to lose solid footing and collapse to the ground. The creature rocked and squirmed, trying to find purchase but couldn't because the legs on the right side of its body dangled over the rocky edge. Solaris roared as she charged the creature and rammed it in the side with her shoulder. It screamed in surprise and snapped at her face. Solaris felt the thing's center of gravity shift, and she dropped down and then pushed up and forward, sending it over the cliff. It squealed all the way down, striking the rocks below.

She stood on the edge of the cliff in shock until a gurgling noise made it to her ears. Solaris spun and located Kotaris behind her. She ran to him, and all she could focus on was the amount of blood he was losing. *Too much.* She stroked his head, wailed and then stroked him again, as he coughed up more of his life fluid. The girl looked at her brother's body; his left arm was crushed and his entire chest was turning purple; there were gouge marks along his rib cage, and blood flowed freely from his mouth. He struggled to catch his breath because of the damage.

Kotaris gargled on his blood, trying to speak, only able to open one eye.

"Shhh. Don't speak," she said, and rested his head on her lap. Solaris could feel convulsive sobs coming, but she did her best to hold them back. "We-we-we'll get you to the house. We can fix it. I can fix it," she whispered as she gingerly touched him.

Sensing her panic, Kotaris lifted his good arm to her face and ran one of his fingers down her cheek…as she used to do to him when he would hurt himself. Solaris grabbed his hand and pressed it hard against her tear-soaked cheek.

"S-s-safe?" he asked.

"Yeah, Ko," she said, running her free hand through his hair. "I'm safe."

"La-love…you," he said, and somehow managed a smile through the pain. Then his eyes closed.

"Ko…," she whispered. "Ko…Kotaris…Kotaris!" she yelled and shook him, letting his arm fall to the ground. "Kotaris!"

Solaris lost her composure. She couldn't deal with the situation anymore and released a scream that woke the dead. The loss of her parents and her brother was just too much—especially her brother.

"No," she screamed. "I was supposed to take care of you. Me! Me!"

"It's over," said a deep, masculine voice.

Solaris looked up through tear filled eyes. She had no doubt, the man before her was the leader she had seen earlier. The man murdered her mother, her father and her brother. He looked down at her over his nose, not even paying her the respect to square off. His face was rigid and weathered, scarred, the look of a hardened monster.

"Time's up," he said, as he grabbed her chin and turned her head to the left and then right. "You'll sell well. Too bad for me you don't have sisters."

Solaris jerked her head from his hands and squeezed her brother tighter. *I won't let them take me.* She looked up into the man's dark eyes. *Not alive. I'll jump from the cliff before I'll be taken.* Solaris looked down at her brother's mangled body and started to position it in a more respectable manner but stopped as she began sobbing. The man continued to ask her questions, but the sound of the beast crunching far below kept playing over and over in her mind. She could do it; she was sure of it. *There is nothing for me now.* Solaris pulled her brother's upper body off the ground and hugged him, resting her face on his bloody shoulder.

"Take her," the captain said.

"No," begged Solaris but his men were already atop her, a large hand on each of her arms. They pulled her away from her brother as she thrashed and screamed, "Wait! Wait! I'll make a deal!"

The long-haired man held up his hand, and his men relaxed their grip. The man snorted and raised an eyebrow at her. "What could you have to offer me?"

"A trade," she sobbed.

"Keep going."

"My brother," she screamed. "I want to take care of him!"

The man looked down at her brother's body and then back up to her. "What do you have to offer?"

Solaris stared at the man in silence, her lip trembling. The leader only waited for a brief moment and then he gestured for them to take her away.

"No," she screamed. "More girls! I'll give you more girls!"

"Stop," he commanded. "Release her."

The men did as they were told and dropped her to the ground. She fell to the dirt and then scrambled over to her brother. After she reached his body, she drew her limbs in, tucking her knees into her body, hiding her face behind them.

"I see honor does not fall off the tree at all," he said as he slowly approached her.

She ignored him. "Let me pay my last respects to my brother and I will show you where they live."

"You'll sell out your people for a few moments with your dead brother?"

Solaris peered over her knees at the man. "Yes."

The captain abruptly turned, seizing her arm around the bicep and her brother around his ankle. He dragged them a short span away from the cliff and then turned Kotaris's leg loose. He flung her onto the ground beside him, but before she could turn to get up, she felt his knee in her back and watched as a black shape slipped across her face and wedged itself between her teeth. She felt straps tighten down across the back of her head and then heard a click. The pressure came off her back, and she flipped over.

"It's so you don't bite your fucking tongue off. It probably wouldn't kill you anyway, but I really don't like to damage my merchandise." The captain pointed at two of his men and motioned for them to stand behind her. They followed his orders, standing between her and the edge of the cliff. She was trapped. He walked a short distance away, turned to watch her, and crossed his arms.

"Remember, more girls. If you lie, you suffer," he said and smiled. "Get on with it, girl."

Solaris straightened her brother's body across the ground, doing her best to fold his arms across his chest. She brushed his hair back over his head, carefully pulling the strands off his face. She searched the ground until she found two suitable leaves and then she placed one leaf over each eye. She could see him well; the moon was full and bright. It seemed to highlight every bruised and battered part of his body. *La-love...you,* echoed his voice in her mind. Solaris buried her face into Kotaris's chest and gave a long wail. Her crying eventually turned into heavy sobs, with each inhale causing a sharp pain in her chest.

She held him and cried, her face on his shoulder. Solaris's emotions bounced between anger and torment. The sharp pain persisted against her breast, and she screamed with frustration, reached under her shirt and yanked the pendant free. She started to throw the necklace to the side, but instead, she lay her head back down onto her brother's shoulder. Her eyes fell upon the pendant in her hand and ran along the length of the pointed end. She opened her hand and studied the pendant. Solaris sucked in a shaky breath as she noticed just how long the pendant was, much longer than she remembered it being. Long enough to do damage.

Solaris sat up and wiped the tears from her cheeks with the back of her free hand. The effort was futile as more tears replaced the ones removed. She straightened her clothing, being sure to keep the pendant out of sight. *Here's one last song for you, Ko. I love you,* she thought. The young woman closed her eyes and began to sing Kotaris's favorite verse:

> "Fall and float, die to go,
> carried on the wind to the world below.

With handless key, and bravest heart,

shall you find the doors will part.

It's their world of slowing time,

those strongest souls left behind.

Bow your head, embrace the key,

you have entered a gods' eternity."

At the end of her song, she threw her head back, exposing her neck. Tears streamed down her cheeks in rivulets as she readied the pendant in her hand. *I'll never let them take me. I will never be a slave to anyone!* She heard one of the men shout, "Stop her," and a heavy hand pressed onto her back, pushing her toward the ground. Instinctively, her arms shot out to brace herself. This caused her to turn the dagger end of the pendant toward her body. In the split second it was happening, her racing mind recognized the opportunity, but time was too limited for her to carefully position it—only seconds to place the pendant with hopes of falling on it effectively. As Solaris felt the man pushing her, he fell too and brought all his weight atop her. The pendant missed her throat by a wide margin and found her chest. She felt the sharpness of the crystal grind against bone and into her heart. The sensation caused her to take in a sharp, shallow breath.

I'm coming, she thought. She rolled over

onto her side, gasping. She pulled her hand away and stared at the dark blood. A strong grip seized her shoulder and rolled her over. The pain had become so intense, it took away most of her external awareness. She was zeroed in on it. The sensation was sharp, and it shot through her entire body with each beat of her heart, electrifying every physical sensation she had. Despite this, she was vaguely aware that the humans were kneeling beside her, probing her wound. Someone lifted her head and shouted at her. Strength had already abandoned her as she lay prostrate in the alien's arms. Eventually, they let her head fall back to the ground. A sudden dull sensation racked the side of her ribs, and she wondered if someone had kicked her.

Darkness was creeping in around the edges of her field of view. *I'm coming*, she thought. Images of her family danced across her mind's eye, and a weak smile spread across her face. The humans had resumed standing over her and talking, but she was unable to comprehend what they were saying. She could hear their strange noises, but the meaning became muddled when it hit her mind. The one in charge, the one called Captain, was red faced and shouting. She felt her heart lurch, the darkness withdrew momentarily, and then it began creeping inward even further. She exhaled slowly as the pain in her chest disappeared. Something clapped loudly, and a brilliant flash pierced her vision. Almost immediately after, something fell on her legs. It was very heavy, but she was too tired and weak to attempt pushing it away. Her confused mind imagined a tree had fallen on her, but she rejected the vision after a few seconds. Solaris wasn't sure what fell on her or when it had precisely. Did it happen before or after the loud noise? It didn't matter anymore. Within seconds, she had already moved beyond any concern for the weight on her legs. She could no longer feel the pressure. Her body was growing cold, as if she was laying on ice. Solaris gasped for air, but only seemed to draw in half of what she would normally. The humans' movements slowed until they stopped altogether.

Suddenly, her body shuddered; her vision seemed to improve, but then her world went dark.

CHAPTER 5

For a time, darkness comprised her entire world. True darkness. Darkness of her entire sense spectrum. Then mental vertigo hit her hard and derailed her mind. This sent her consciousness drifting into a world of peaceful incomprehension. She wasn't aware, that she wasn't aware of what was happening to her. Mind reeling, she struggled to place her position; her lifeforce was being pulled in all directions, and at the same time, all of existence was being drawn into her soul. Solaris wasn't sure how she connected the feeling with traveling, but she became more certain as her mind accessed its sensors again.

First, the ability to hear came back to her, the majority of it consisted of air rushing past her ears with the occasional whip-snap of loose clothing. Her nostrils flared as a strong scent struck her, river water. The scent triggered a memory of her running through a dew laden field as a child. A man chased her across the field, and she was laughing. Solaris smiled, the memory filling her with joy. She basked in the comfort of that recollection until she realized her mouth was dry. She felt the thirst more keenly as she noticed how cool and damp the air was; it slipped in-between the open areas of her clothing, sending goosebumps across her skin.

She remained level as her body moved through the void, arms and legs gently bobbing against the up swell of rushing air. Solaris tried opening her eyes, but the lids wouldn't budge. They felt welded together, refusing to be pried apart. She continued this way for an indeterminate amount of time. She was calm until she heard the crack of a gunshot. Her ease evaporated, and a cold chill raced through her body as her mind groped for the memory of what birthed the feeling but was unable to retrieve it. Her thoughts were disjointed, impossible to direct, impossible to understand. As her mind wandered, it brought forth images of events she could not escape seeing. Some of them disturbed her greatly. There was one of an armored human standing over her with a gun. She couldn't place his face, but he was familiar. His presence was a physical weight on her chest threatening to crush her. She felt heat rise into her cheeks, and her breath quickened as the man reached down, his long fingers spreading across her view.

Solaris jerked, yelling *no* into the darkness,

fleeing from his grasp. Images rapidly swirled, solidified and disappeared. She clawed the darkness when the images were disturbing and relaxed when they were pleasant, floating in the air as if suspended in water.

Most of the pleasant visions were of the same three people. A beautiful woman with a silk touch and a kiss as soft as a summer cloud. A man whose words she could not understand, but whose voice brought a warm blanket of comfort. And the last was a young man whose arms were solid, her shield. Solaris held him tight, locking her fingers around his waist so he couldn't vanish, but she knew he would. He was going to leave her because he had no choice. He was gone, and he had to go. Her grip tightened around him as one second stretched into another and then her arms collapsed through the air.

Gone.

Solaris held herself, screamed in terror and agony, the tormented sound echoing around her. Tears leaked from her eyes and rolled down her cheeks until the wind caught them. It carried them upwards with the draft, defying gravity. She clung to herself and the vision of those three people until it slipped from her, like water slips through a clenched fist. As the connection to the flow of images severed, she also was losing all awareness of self, reverting to a more primal state of mind.

She fought this change, trying to focus her thoughts on concepts of the what and where of her immediate surroundings but found it futile. Eventually, her mind settled into a state of persistent unease. She found she could hold onto that. Something was wrong, and she needed to be wary. She might need to fight or maybe run, but she couldn't know quite yet.

The cool wind rushing over her slowed, then stopped, and her backside was tickled by hundreds of strands of grass. The grass was soft, providing a natural cushion for her to lay on, and the other strands surrounding her body stood straight and tall trying to conceal her position. She wanted to get up and run her fingers through the grass and feel it beneath her feet, but the unconscious knowledge of how to move was locked away in her mind. Solaris summoned as much will as she could and only managed to grasp weakly at strands of nearby grass. Then she would stop for a time and only exist. She didn't forget what she was trying to do; it was more that she just stopped caring shortly after she attempted to investigate.

Many cycles of this passed as Solaris lay on her back, dreaming, somewhere between a second and eternity, but she refused to give up, and eventually, she was rewarded as her heavy lids obeyed and opened.

Solaris gasped in astonishment, half because she was able to see, and half because of what she saw—the alignment of several unfamiliar moons in the sky. There were five of them, the largest of which was blue, then red, green, yellow and black. The yellow moon was close to the blue moon, orbiting around it. They were all positioned around each other but not necessarily positioned because of each other.

The gasp tickled her throat, and she coughed. Then she tried to swallow and found that her mouth was very dry. *Green Mother, I'm thirsty—what was that?* There was a noise, a twig snapped due to a shifting of weight nearby. *Someone's here*, she thought.

"Interesting," it said. The force of the masculine voice traveled through the ground, vibrating the gravel beneath her hands. "No one has dared approach my solemn gate in an age. I don't know whether to be impressed or insulted you came by yourself." The words were so powerful they caused pressure inside her ears to fluctuate. "So young to be without a Hadagii Elken. So vulnerable. So sweet…"

Titanic footfalls stomped toward her, and the racket of heavy clanking metal filled the air; Solaris recognized it as the sound of moving chains, but then thought it impossible due to how heavy they sounded. The chains would have to be close to the size of the ones used to anchor the cargo ships in the port of the great river. No living creature could carry such weight.

The mysterious presence eased to a stop, staying just out of her view and gave a long exhale, its hot, misty breath cascading over her body.

Solaris shivered and tried to inch away from the snort but couldn't get her body to coordinate enough to do so. She quickly scanned her surroundings to find the source of the voice, where exactly she was, and a way out.

The distant horizons were overcast with brightly colored clouds, leading her to believe either dawn or dusk was upon them, but she couldn't be sure which. Her sense of time was unanchored. She searched the sky, realizing she had regained more ability to move her head, but just that small increase in movement was taxing. She wasn't tired from the movement, just unable to keep moving. *Okay, Solaris,* she thought. *Figure out where you are.*

To all sides were living walls; enormous dark-green needled trees stood side-by-side. Most of them were covered in moss that was littered with small blue flowers. Little was visible beyond the gnarled trunks of the trees, only a misty darkness between the gaps punctuated by light filtering down through an occasional hole in the canopy. The air was hazy with an orange-tinted mist, and she could feel her dampened clothes clinging to her body. Giant stone obelisks surrounded her position, maybe seven or eight. It was hard for her to tell without being able to look around clearly. She watched the nearest stone and realized it moved. The giant stone bobbed gently up and down, never touching the ground and never flying away.

Solaris tried to move her body again but was still unable to make it respond fully to her commands. Her muscles now flinched when she urged them to move, but that was it. Having somewhat established her whereabouts, it became painfully obvious the being was waiting on a response, but she wasn't sure what to say. He hadn't made his intentions clear with her, so she was reluctant to tell him anything, but she knew there was a malice about him—the aura of a dark stranger skulking in the shadow of an alley. Solaris tried to formulate an appropriate response, but she was having a hard time coming up with anything she felt was remotely suitable. Her mind was sluggish from her deep sleep state.

"Hello," she said tilting her head toward the direction of the raspy breath.

"You are different than the last Hadagii that came through my gate."

"Am I?"

"Yes," it grumbled. "Very."

"I...I can't move. Can you help me? I'm sorry, what's your name?"

It sucked in a quick breath which Solaris interpreted as surprise. "What a dangerous question to ask. Who I am...well figuring that out is your burden," it trailed off, growing silent. She wished she could hear it thinking while she listened to the deep whoosh of its breath come in and then out, slow and steady. "I am aware you cannot move. It always happens to the new pilgrims. And it depends."

"Depends on what? Where am I?"

The creature laughed harshly. "If you keep this up, we will be dining together tonight. You are in the place between light and dark. The beginning and the end. Armatoran."

The last word was familiar to her, but she couldn't place its exact meaning. *Isn't that from one of the stories that Grandma told me?*

"What?" she muttered. She felt her chest tighten with panic as she was unable to process exactly what was happening to her. *Why can't I move,* she thought. *Where am I?* The being was laughing again. The noise he made was as far from sounding joyful as water was from being dry. It was then—as her mind still recovering—she knew she had become the prey.

"Your name. Your people," it demanded. "And mine?"

"I am Solaris of the Urokos. I don't know your name. I've already asked you who you are."

He paced around her, back and forth, but always out of her line of sight. On his last pass, he came in close, and she felt something smooth slide across her right shoulder. The sudden touch caused her to flinch, and she cried out. Solaris's heart began pumping into overdrive, and her breathing turned erratic. She quickly governed it back under control, drawing in-and-out through flared nostrils.

Her response excited him; he growled and clawed at the dirt. She could feel and smell his breath on the side of her face and neck. It was the odor of pungent swamp and the rot of meat. He sniffed her again in great long draws, nudging her head in the process. Her eyes bounced around her field of vision, desperately searching for him, but he was too sly and remained out of sight.

"That's once. I'll give you some more time to think while you answer my other questions. Let no one ever say I have no honor. You do not smell like the Hadagii. Why did you come here?" it growled.

She searched her memories but could not find an answer. *How did I get here? Why can't I remember?* She wanted to answer with a general response but knew deep down, only one answer was correct. Solaris took a moment to force her mind to focus.

She was certain her interrogator wasn't

there to help and wouldn't. The edge in his voice was too harsh. Too demanding. Too intense. It reminded her of a time she had been with her father while he met with some humans in their embassy. Instead of staying in the waiting room, she had snuck off and run right into a human security guard, but quick thinking and name dropping kept her from being detained. And just like that situation, one wrong word could shift the outcome. But unlike that situation, she knew there was much more at stake.

Okay. Okay. I know who the Hadagii are, but what do they have to do with him? I don't...why can't I remember anything. What the hell is going on?

Her muscles tensed, and she felt a lump push to the top of her throat. *Calm down, Solaris. Think. Give him something.* She tried to speak and remembered her mouth was very dry. She couldn't remember the last time she had a drink. Solaris swallowed and rolled her tongue around. It did little good.

Wait, he said something about a gate. Didn't someone used to tell me some story about Armatoran and Gate Guardians? But that's...there is no way this is about to work. "You do not smell like Hadagii either, and I came to see the Gate Guardian. That's what you are," she said.

The thing huffed and she could hear it shifting its weight from one foot to the other. The movement sent chills across her body as she put together how large it must be to shake the ground with such force. "You don't smell of lies, but no one comes to this gate to see me, girl. Hadagii avoid this gate. Even Hadagii Elken will not brave an encounter with me. That must mean you don't remember what brings you here. I had hoped for a little conversation at least, but your mind must still be recuperating from crossing Siluk's web. What of the Hadagii? Has their order fallen to time?"

"What?" she asked. *I need to keep him talking. Find out what's going on.* "Order? No, I don't think so. There are lots of Hadagii in my valley. What... what do Hadagii have to do with me?"

"There are four gates for fah'dienh into Armatoran, including mine. Not one traveler has braved my gate for over an eon. The last was a Hadagii Elken—Rhathal, curse him—and he vowed to seal the entrance to my gate forever. I believed his vow accomplished until now, but you're no Hadagii. So, if the Hadagii didn't send you...you must have been claimed by a key. I wonder who sent you? How did you fall?"

"What?"

"How did you die, girl?"

The start of a word escaped her mouth and then another, before she whispered, "I died." Her response was somewhere between a question and affirmation. It was in that moment that her memories returned in a visual flood, and the color drained from her face.

"I see it comes back to you now. Good that your mind is not shattered. Tell me how you died," he said and then she could feel him leaning in toward her. Suddenly, it made a sharp noise—a bark and a cough. "Waaaait. That smell. I have not crossed that scent for quite some time. You are not dead. You are Mestagorii?" it questioned.

She could hear a sharp tone enter its voice, and he sounded affable for once. It made her very uneasy. "Impossible! That is old magic!"

"What? I don't understand," she pleaded. An involuntary shudder rumbled through her body.

The being roared and snorted. "Mestagorii!" it said. "I have waited a long time for a visitor, but I never thought I would see the likes of you. Luck is with me. I watched you lay in this field for nearly a day. Fending off those that prowl and howl, fulfilling my Yasubi. But now, I know I am blessed to be in the presence of a Mestagorii. After I consume you, your soul's living connection to Grea will help sustain me for quite a span. I can't remember the last time I wasn't starving."

"Consume me?" she whispered.

It snorted and made a deep rumbling noise. "Yeeeeeeeeeeees," it said and then she heard a great snapping noise beside her head and realized it was the sound of many teeth clacking. "Let's be done with this, as the only good here is for you to satisfy *me*, conversation be damned. No prowler is going to come by and take you from me. I am the Guardian of the South Gate. Again, speak my name to pass or take one step closer to becoming one with me. Answer, Mestagorii!"

She tried looking behind her, but was unable too, though she did turn just a little. Her eyes swept over the sky, from one edge of the tree line to the other. The shape of the clearing triggered a memory deep in her mind.

She must have been only four or five years old at the time. There was a campfire and a skinny, elderly man standing over it. He stomped around the fire clamping his arms up and down mimicking scissors and then held up outstretched fingers to his head—crooked antlers. Then the memory flashed to him holding up three fingers before he charged one of the children sitting cross-legged around the fire and pretended to eat him with his arms.

She could see the old man stop his actions and look at her. His mouth was moving. Repeating something, but she couldn't remember it.

"Answer!"

"I do not know," she screamed, and a tear ran down her cheek. "Please don't eat me!"

"By the Seven Hands will, I am bound to ask you one more time. What am I called?" She felt the creature come in close again, the stench of its breath rolling over her body.

"No. No," she wailed. "I don't know. Please!"

"I am Bakuun," it said. "I have granted three chances, and you have failed them all. Your life is mine." She felt something dig under the ground and then lift her into the air. As she ascended, she saw one massive, furry finger close over her face, blocking out her vision. She dangled helplessly as the beast repositioned her through the air. She could feel gravity shift as it turned her over. *Green Mother*, she thought. *It's eating me!*

Cold fear raced down her back and burrowed into her stomach. She reacted—the surge of emotion breaking the spell that immobilized her —kicked her legs out, looking for purchase. Her right foot slid down something long and slick, and the left planted firmly into something soft. She pressed hard against the surface, trying to prevent herself from going any further.

"Don't eat me!"

The creature growled and snapped her to the side, causing her legs to lay flat against his palm so he could pin them with the rest of his fingers. As this happened, she shifted and caught a glimpse of the outside world—rows of teeth. All she could focus on were canines as long as her

90

arms and the dark hole of a throat that could swallow a small vehicle.

She lost all her composure then and screamed with all her might. Solaris squirmed in its grip, trying to break free, but only managed to get one of her arms loose. She pushed on the massive finger, covering the top of her face, but Bakuun was too strong and large. For all her effort, she couldn't budge the log sized digit. Solaris tried escaping, which amounted to little more than wiggling her feet and slapping at the creature's giant fingers. She descended this way until a bright pink flash of light erupted across her vision.

She sensed her momentum stop, heard Bakuun grunt, and then felt his fingers part, opening a gap across her chest. The movement of his massive index finger pushed and twisted her head so far beyond its normal range, she was sure any more pressure, and her skull was going to come loose from her body. Suddenly, the world turned upright again, and she dropped down a span. Something hard clinked against her chest, and she felt vibrations spread across her ribcage.

"This cannot be," it growled.

The pressure from its index finger eased off her head, and she screamed, "Let me go!"

"All these years...?" Bakuun asked.

Solaris continued to scream and press against his fingers.

"No wonder I couldn't find it. It was in Grea the whole time...and now it's on you—in you. How did this happen?"

Solaris hadn't stopped screaming and resisting him since he eased off, and she didn't care to answer any of his questions.

Bakuun slipped his index finger down and then rolled it up slightly until it pinned her bottom jaw shut. He left just enough room so she could peer over his knuckle and see him. Solaris stopped struggling and screaming because it was all she could do not to piss herself.

The creature's skull was the size of a cargo transport vehicle. Black spiked antlers adorned both sides of his head, each four times longer than she was tall. He was covered in dark grey fur and equipped with a short muzzle filled with massive canines. His six green eyes all stared at her, unblinking, and glowing; the irises swirled with strands of bright green energy—they held the presence of vibrant, uncontrollable life. The longer she looked into his eyes, the more she felt herself slipping...being lured into a trance. In that last instant of their connection, she felt their minds touch.

She could feel him—not just physically—but on a level she had never experienced before. For a fraction of a moment, she connected her mind to his emotions. She could feel all the hate, anguish, desperation, and unfulfilled desire for revenge roiling through his mind. Then all six of his brows furrowed, severing her link to him.

"I've had enough of your screaming, and if it wasn't for that key, you'd already be ground up and on-the-way down. Heed me. I wonder if the risk of eating you is less than the benefit of having peace and quiet? Do we understand each other?"

She thought of no reason why she should even try to defy him. His size alone was intimidating enough, but her perception of his intent was crystal clear. As he spoke, she knew he meant what he said—he was going to eat her if she didn't stop.

Solaris nodded her head.

The creature released a tame grunt, and he lowered her back down into the misty grass. He paused for a moment, locking eyes with her as if he were going to say something and then turned away.

She watched his massive, clawed fingers uncurl and felt them gently slide out from underneath her. Although she was sure she could move, she dared not do so.

She wanted to believe that her recent past was just a dream. She would wake up any moment to Kotaris standing over her, shaking her awake. It would be time for dinner and then she would be able to sit around the table and tell her parents all about the nightmare she had. About the creature that wanted to eat her but couldn't. That's what she wanted it to be but knew it wasn't.

The cold of the dew dampening the clothes that stuck to her body was real. The stiff bristles of the creature's fur sliding against her bare skin was real. The death of her family was real. *This world is real,* she thought. *Armatoran exists. Grandma's stories...she knew. How could she know about this place?*

After the last of Bakuun's fingers pulled out from underneath her, she squeezed her eyes closed and thanked the Green Mother for her protection. Solaris listened to the creature back away, noticed the loud thrash of displaced branches as he pushed his way through nearby trees. Then there was a large thump followed by a miniature earthquake.

Solaris curled into a ball and tried to force her mind to go blank—but it rebelled—forcing her to process what was happening and what had happened. She turned onto her side and curled into a fetal position, tucking her face into her arms, tears flowing freely. What was she going to do? Everyone was dead and she was alone in a nightmare world.

A lump formed in her throat as she sobbed, causing her to cough. When she finished, she screamed and struck the ground with her fist. The motion, caused a tear to split off from the others and roll down the end of her nose, tickling her. She wiped it away, her forearm brushing an alien object on her chest. She brought her hand back up, investigating the new attachment. *What is that?*

Where the wound should have been, she found the smoothness of metal splayed across bare skin. Solaris tucked her chin into look downward. Upon her chest and embedded off center was the pendant, though it no longer held its original shape. The only familiarity was the crystal in the center of the emblem. *This is the key he was talking about?*

The trinket no longer held any resemblance to a dagger but branched out in various directions across her chest in a symmetrical fashion. It resembled the roots of a tree now. She had no memory of how or when the addition became a part of her. Solaris gingerly pressed on the object and realized it was sensitive as if a part of her—painless and very warm. Her mind wandered back to her recent memory of being trapped in Bakuun's grasp and contemplated if the object on her chest had been the source of the light and heat.

"Stand, Mestagorii," said the creature.

His command brought her thoughts back to the present situation. She owed it to her family to try and survive, and that was what she was going to do. She was given a second chance, after all. Solaris traced the pendant with her fingertips, wondering how the key brought her there, where it would bring her next. Satisfied there were no answers to be had at that moment, she turned onto her stomach to face Bakuun. There would be time to figure out what exactly the key was later. For now, it seemed to afford her some modicum of protection—at least from the beast—and that was enough.

Solaris pushed her upper body up, just high enough to peer over the tall grass. At first, she couldn't discern anything but trees, large boulders and undergrowth. Then a shifting bulk came into view from within the depths of the darkness. Solaris fixed her gaze on the lumbering shadow with six green, glowing eyes. From the outline of his body, she could see he was sitting on a large boulder. The beast rubbed his face, pulling at the small mane under its chin.

"Get off the ground little Grean rabbit," it grumbled. "Have you no sense of honor? Dinner will not be served tonight. Besides, you're not but bones…painful on the way out."

Solaris blurted, "You ask about honor? Where is yours, monster? Skulking in the woods and eating people!" Her hand came up to her mouth as an afterthought, much too late to stop anything.

The creature laughed. It was deep and dark, vibrating the ground underneath her. Joy was absent from the sound it made.

"I see you have grit…good. But no honor? I am the physical manifestation of honor!" It huffed and then jumped to its feet; the sudden movement sent vibrations running through the ground and up her legs. "I've ripped battalions apart with my bare claws. Wedged myself between armies and crushed them all! Braved the pits of Urlankai and resurfaced with my life and in the same night sparred the foolish paupers who would dare approach me for a handout. Never have I knelt or begged for anything! I am Bakuun! Bakuun the Crusher! Bakuun the Devourer! Bakuun--,"

"The bound," she shouted, fists clinched at her sides. A voice. No, not a voice. Some presence whispered at the fringes of her mind and imbued her with the understanding that this creature would no longer try and eat her, even though he might threaten to. That made her confident the creature wouldn't even harm her. *Besides, who the hell was he to talk to her that way? Who just wakes up in the middle of nowhere and knows where they are? Or know who he was? Self-centered bastard*, she thought.

Her certainty ran bold and strong until the coldness of his eyes registered in her mind. As this happened, a chill ran up her spine and seeded doubt about him not being able to harm her.

The creature uncoiled, straightening up to its full height, its bright emerald eyes flaring like searing embers. He swiped violently at a tree that stood between him and her, toppling it with ease. She watched in awe as the giant stared down upon her, mountainous, feral and unblinking. She felt he was probably the largest living creature she had ever laid eyes on, definitely the largest she had ever seen standing on two legs.

Solaris hoped his aggression against the tree would satisfy his desire to lash out at her, but she knew that was a long shot. Before she could respond to diffuse the situation, his short-lived silence gave way to a flourishing growl. The growl escalated, growing louder and more aggressive until it evolved into a blasting roar—the sound so harsh, she had to cover her ears with her hands. Ancient trees collapsed; birds took to the sky, and her vision went out of focus as his bellow rattled her entire body.

Solaris dared not remove her eyes from the monster. She had angered him, and now, he had changed his mind, decided to come to finish the job he had started before. Bakuun shutdown his roar and looked to his left and then his right before bending over to wrap himself around a tree. The bright light of the moons cascaded over his body, highlighting the large bundles of muscles contracting over his shoulder and back. He grunted; the trunk of the tree cracked loudly and then the pointed tip of the tree suddenly lurched into the sky. Solaris sucked in an anxious breath as she recognized an audible *hmph* of effort just before the massive tree was soaring through the air like a spear. It was hurtling straight for her.

The tree soared across the clearing, momentarily blocking out the alignment of moons. She almost bolted, but the voice in her head told her to hold her ground, and she would be safe so long as she didn't move. She held fast, planting her feet to the dirt and clenching her fingers into tight fists. Solaris closed her eyes, slightly turning her head as the tree came crashing down.

Leaves slapped her across the face; the earth erupted and spewed debris, dust, and vegetation into the air. She recoiled, bringing her hands up to protect herself but refused to move her feet. Solaris waited, eyes closed, fists full of some material. Time passed, and she realized she was holding her breath. She let it out and then took in a long, slow draw through her nose, opened one eye and then the next.

A massive tree, nearly five times larger around than she was, lay next to her. In her hands were clusters of green leaves. She stared at the tree, taking in how large it was, until the creature broke the silence.

"A pity you didn't move. Well, there's that grit again," it grumbled and then she watched some of the tension slip from its shoulders. "And aye, I am bound you, bitch. Bound beyond your judgement or understanding. Bound to a nature that others construe as a necessary evil. If you knew who I was, you would not be so quick to loosen your tongue. Disrespectful Grea walker."

Solaris stared at the tree next to her a moment longer and then she turned to the creature, feeling heat race into her face. This thing was playing a game with her. It was then she realized if she had moved the wrong way, the tree would have crushed her, and it would have technically been her fault because she would have stepped into its path. Bakuun never intended to throw it at her current position—he threw it hoping she would step into the line of fire.

When she realized this, part of her wanted to sprint as far away as she could from him, but the overwhelming majority of her being wished she could pick up the tree and hurl it back at him. "Disrespectful?" she shouted. "Child," she followed and took a shaky step forward. "You tried to eat me!"

The creature snatched its head to the right, "Bah..." The noise thundered across the expanse.

"Why did you try to eat me?"

"I am bound to fulfil my Yasubi, bound by compulsion."

"I don't believe you, but how does that even make it right?" she shouted with her hands in the air.

The creature remained quiet for a moment and then continued. "You speak of fairness…you will find none here. Others do not carry the curse of my compulsion. I am required to follow a set of rules, however minor. And don't be lulled by that damn key; it will not protect you from everything. Speaking of which, I wonder…," it said, trailing off and then gestured into the air.

A high-pitched scream came from behind her. She spun and was confronted by a ghost charging her with an outstretched, withered hand. Before she had time to react, the thing's hand plunged into her chest, followed by its arm, and then the rest of its body. As the essence passed through her, it was like she had been dunked into an ice-cold lake, the experience ripping the air from her lungs, and she tumbled to a knee.

The spirit passed through her and spun upward toward the sky, flares of a tattered dress billowing around its body as it went. The young woman continued to watch the spirit as it raced over to Bakuun and then vanished into the blackness of the creature's face. It seemed Bakuun had actually breathed in the ethereal being just as it reached him. He was quiet for a moment, his green eyes disappeared, and then one-by-one they opened again.

"You have Hadagii blood. It's faint, but it's there, almost like it's being masked. How fortuitous that I didn't eat you. That means we could

101

be of use to each other. Before you scamper off to your doom in the woods beyond, why don't you ask me a question? Save yourself pain and time, and just ask me what you really want to know."

CHAPTER 6

Solaris paused for a moment to think of what she should ask. He was digging for something, pushing her toward some goal he had. If she was dead, was this the afterlife? *But wait, he said I wasn't dead. I'm Mestagorii or whatever that means.* Did that mean she could go back to her world? *Is that what he meant by the pendant being a key?* Why was it attached to her, and why was he so cautious of it? She looked down and fingered the glowing roza crystal embedded in her chest. *What did he mean by cursed by compulsion? Something is forcing him to obey? Forcing him to fulfill a Yasubi... Yasubi. I think I remember one of the Urokos mentioning it before. It being a curse or some kind of a magical compulsion. Then that means there are other magical beings in Armatoran—some even stronger than this demon. Did they have some measure of control over him? I can't believe I'm actually in Armator —.*

"Well," he said baring teeth in a semi-smile.

Do you have your damned question or not? How about home? Do you not want to go back home?"

The same sense that warned her she was in danger earlier told her he was revealing his hand now. This thing was bound to answer her question. She felt it would tell the truth, but wasn't certain to what degree. She knew truth to him rested on a sliding scale. At best, it would only tell the absolute truth for selfish reasons and at worst, to mislead.

"Can you bring my family here?"

He straightened. "What? Why would you want to do that?"

"My brother, mother, and father. I want them back. Can you do that?"

"What do you mean back?"

"A human took them from me. Killed them in front of me," she said. With no warning, a tear pooled and then slid down her cheek. Solaris quickly rubbed it away, not wanting Bakuun to take notice. She didn't want to let him see any more weakness from her.

"I see," he said and narrowed his eyes. "Resurrection is not something I deal with."

"So, you can't help. Or won't?"

"I can help, but not with that."

"Then who can help me?"

"Cowering not five minutes before. Now you stand there and badger me for answers. You asked a question, I answered it. It's done."

"Help," she screamed. "Who can help?" Unable to hold them back, the tears flowed freely down her face and she didn't bother to wipe them this time.

Bakuun looked down and then turned his head far to the side, stretching his neck. It must have popped because he grunted and then turned his attention back onto her. "What you seek is not what you want, but I will tell you anyway. There is a man named Novu that lives along the left side of the cliff in an abandoned monastery. If you follow the red moon it will take you to the cliff. He has the answer you seek. But..."

"Yes?"

"You won't make it. And if you did, you won't like his answer."

"You don't know that. You don't know me."

"I don't need to know you to know you won't make it, girl. Look at this," he said. Bakuun raised his arm and rattled the chain attached to his wrist.

"So, you can't leave. What does that have to do with me?" *I'm tired of this. He's just going to try and talk me out of going so he can use me for something.*

"You still don't get it, do you?" he said. "Why do you think my enslavers left me *here*...in the middle of nowhere?"

Solaris huffed. "It's obvious, you're evil. They put you out here to keep you away from everyone else."

"Look around you. What do you see?"

"I don't have time for your games," she said and turned away. The red moon looked like it was south, or maybe it was north. She really couldn't tell given that it was a totally different sky than what she was used to. Solaris began marching in the direction of the red moon.

"This place is a deathtrap. They didn't put me here to keep me away from everyone else. I'm here so they can keep everyone away from me."

Solaris felt hesitation creep into her mind after Bakuun spoke. She almost slowed down to probe him for more answers but decided against it. *Don't play into his game.* She didn't want to let him believe he had any power over the decision she made. Besides, he was just trying to get into her head.

"Don't go into the woods, girl. We're a week's travel from any civilization and nothing benevolent lives this far out in the black forest. Including Novu."

"I'll take my chances."

"So be it. When you face your death—and you will shortly—don't fight, run."

Solaris marched across the field, ignoring him. She was ready to put some distance between her and that beast. Anywhere else had to be better than near a monster. As she walked close to one of the floating obelisks, she let her hand slide across its surface. The object was warm to the touch and made the hairs on her arm stand up. At first glance, she thought it was just solid rock, but as she looked closer, she could see there were veins of a dark blue crystalline structure running throughout the entire slab. In the center of the rock, facing into the clearing, was the imprint of a hand. She traced her finger along the edge of the imprint and then glanced across the clearing at the other stones. There were seven in total and each had one distinct hand imprint. Solaris let her hand fall away from the stone and then glanced out into the woods.

The woods were horrifyingly dark.

What if Bakuun was telling the truth? What if there was something worse than him out in the woods? She knew what she was doing was crazy, no matter how she tried to rationalize it. She was trusting that there was a helpful magical hadagii that could and would help her. *Nothing benevolent lives this far out,* he had said. At the same time, she was ignoring his warning that death awaited her in the woods. Was it Novu? Was he warning her cryptically?

Maybe the right move was to go home. She wondered if he had some way to actually send her home since he brought it up. *But the way he looked at me when he said that. He wants something. Something that will cost me.* Solaris brought her hand up to her chest and wondered if the stab wound would still be gone if she went back. Would she still have the key? *This could be your one and only chance to bring them back to life. Armatoran is real. That means all the old stories are probably true. True magic exists so someone here can help. If not Novu then someone else. Don't let him get to you. He's a lying demon.* And even if she did make it back, she would have to face the captain and outsmart him. Better to bring her family to her.

So, there were two choices. She could stay in the clearing and die, or she could try. She didn't want to hear out any deal from Bakuun because she knew it was going to be one-sided. If a devil gave you a deal, it was best to just walk away from the game. Solaris decided to press onward. She would scout the area first, only going out a short distance, marking her way as she went and take it slow. If she ran into trouble she could always come back.

She pulled away from the stone and made her way to the woods, but the closer she go to the tree line, the more she began to lose her resolve. She scanned the woods, unable to make out much beyond a stone's throw inside. Then there was a flash of movement off to the right, and Solaris froze, snapping her head in that direction to see what it was. She waited, scanning that area of the tree line until she was satisfied her mind was just playing tricks on her. *Nothing. Nothing is there,* she thought.

She closed her eyes, took a deep breath in, and then let it flow out. *I'm going to find Novu. I'm going to get my family back.* Solaris opened her eyes and resumed walking. When she was within several paces of the edge of the clearing, all the hairs on her body stood up, and a light blue shimmer wavered before her. She stopped to examine it. The light rippled across open space and then rose upward, flowing across some invisible dome. *What is this?* Solaris reached out and raked her fingers through the translucent dome. Again, waves of light flowed outward and upward. *Whatever it is, doesn't hurt.* She turned and looked for Bakuun. He was still sitting in the same spot, watching her with his unblinking green eyes.

Mom. Dad. Ko.

Solaris closed her eyes again and stepped through the semi-visible dome. She expected to feel something happen to her. A jolt of pain or tingling sensation, but nothing happened; it was like it wasn't even there. When she was across, she opened one eye and then the next. *See. You can do it,* she thought. She looked back again, swiping her hand through the air, but this time there were no ripples of energy, no sign that anything mystical existed at all. She was still testing the field of energy, waving her fingers though it when she noticed Bakuun's eyes were gone. Curious, she took a step forward and Bakuun materialized. She took a step back, and he disappeared again.

I'm here so they can keep everyone away from me, he had said. *There is some kind of spell here; it hides him—hides this place. Who could be so bad that complete, hidden isolation was the only answer? Why didn't they just kill him?* She gave the creature one final glance, hoped he was lying about the dangers beyond, and then turned away. *I'm not staying here.*

The trees appeared large when she first noticed them earlier, but now that she was standing before them, she realized large was an understatement. Some of them were as wide as she was tall, natural monsters. The misty forest was imposing with its ancient, gnarled guardians, creeping roots, wide reaching branches with webs of thick vines, and infestation of moss strands that ran down to the dirt. They reminded her of long, grey beards, except for the glow.

The grey clumps of moss were peppered with blue flowers. The flowers were tiny, but each one gave off a powerful pale blue light and together they emitted an eerie glow. She scooped up a handful of the tangled mess to examine it more closely. The entire flower didn't glow, just the pistil. For a moment, she smiled as she imagined Ko-taris plucking off one of the flora to eat it and then her smile evaporated. She let the clump fall from her hand and concentrated on the way before her. Hundreds of individual strands of ghostly blue moss hung from the tops of trees and stopped just short of scraping the ground. *At least they will provide some light along the way,* she thought.

The undergrowth was thick with low lying bushes, broad frond ferns, and stalks of red-leafed weeds. The earth rolled and dipped gently, and it was covered with cast foliage, shed branches, and a light mist that flowed out of the forest and into the clearing. The light breeze that rolled over her brought the scents of dried leaves, a sweet, flowery smell, and the cleanness of winter air.

Solaris stood at the edge, rubbing her hands together and then blew into them. The air was much colder near the tree-line.

She rubbed her arms and then stomped with frustration at the change in temperature. When her foot came down it struck something hard. She examined the ground but couldn't make anything out so she probed with the back of her heel, kicking the dirt and grass away. *Stop stalling and just go. Everyone's relying on you.*

Solaris looked up from her excavation and found the red moon, peaking over the edge of the treetops. *How am I going to follow that if I can't see it? I guess I'll walk as straight as I can until I find a break in the canopy. And if I don't find one, then I'll just have to climb up a tree and find it after I've covered some ground.*

She waited at the edge for a span, holding her arms and thinking about what Bakuun said. Death trap. Part of her wanted to turn back to him and ask if he was being honest with her. Maybe he was? He could be honest and a monster, couldn't he? He could be interested in her safety so he could use her in the future for some diabolical reason. *Or there could be help just a short hike away, and he's just lying to you. You can do it, Solaris. You've grown up in the jungle and know how to survive. Who's he to tell you that you won't make it?*

She scanned the darkness, swallowed and pushed into the woods. She took one step and then another, feeling the crunch of leaves and snap of twigs beneath her feet, slipping past groping vines and moss beards. It wasn't long before she had walked far enough that the clearing behind her was no longer in sight. The darkness around her seemed to be alive, coating everything like oil despite the light blue glow of the flowers that punctuated it. However, she discovered a new-found talent.

The pendant that had become part of her gave off a soft, pink glow. It was enough light for her to see a few paces in any direction. Once she figured out that she had a built-in flashlight, she

112

tore the collar off of her shirt to open a space for the crystal to cast light unimpeded.

The brush was thick, which she thought was odd given there was so little light. Back home in the jungle, most of the undergrowth was thickest when the trees were sparse. *This is a different world, she thought. There must be different rules.* She turned and gazed at where she had pushed through. *At least if I need to find my way back to the clearing, I should be able to find it.* Mostly out of training but partially due to nervousness, she had intentionally left herself a return trail. As she pushed deeper, she grabbed long strands of the glowing moss and tied them into a loop. If the worst happened, and she needed to run, she should be able to follow the loops all the way back to the clearing. All the way back to Bakuun, who may or may not help her.

Part of her still believed Bakuun was telling her the truth, but the further in she went, the less she believed him. She hadn't crossed paths with a single creature larger than a bird since her departure, but several times, she did hear something making some kind of warbling noise in the distance. She was heading away from the sound, so she tried not to conjure up any images of what it might be.

Solaris crossed over a fallen log and stopped as she reached a small drop off before a winding creek. The creek wasn't particularly wide, but it did look deep in certain parts. How deep, was impossible to know due to the darkness. It would be best to avoid those areas she identified as suspiciously absent of protruding stones. The water flowed lazily, spilling over and around smooth rocks breaching the surface. *Finally! I am so thirsty.*

She scanned the small beach for any threats. There were no creatures or tracks that she could tell. No carcasses or skeletons left near the water's edge, and the embankment wasn't steep enough to create an issue in the event she needed to escape.

Solaris hiked down the embankment and stepped across a couple of stones in the water so she could draw a drink away from the sandy bank. She squatted down and scooped up a handful of water, analyzing it for a moment, concerned about what would happen if the liquid was turned.

On one hand, if she didn't drink when it was available, she ran the risk of not finding another source before it was too late, and she could tell her body was in need of hydration. However, if it was foul and ran her stomach, she would dehydrate even faster and risk possible death if she couldn't find help.

Stop scaring yourself. This isn't stagnant water, she thought. *It shouldn't be any different than home. There is no trash anywhere and I don't think pollution is a problem here.*

She brought the water up to her nose and detected no alarming odors. Most of it had spilled from her hand, but she let what remained fall into her dry, parched mouth. So good. It was cold and clean. She scooped a second amount and then drank again, and again, continuing the process until she'd had her fill.

She let a sigh escape her lips and traced a playful finger in the water as she thought about where she was going. Bakuun never told her how long it would take to reach the cliff, only that she needed to keep following the red moon. *There's less trees here, maybe I can see it?* She looked up and found it peeking through weak holes in the canopy. *There you are*, she thought and then she jerked her attention back down as something brushed her finger. She pulled her hand away, breath caught in her chest and heart pounding.

Where her finger had been, a long, thin object now protruded from the water. It was thin like an antenna and drooped at the end. She stared at it, frozen with focus and then relaxed into a smile. It was just a piece of water grass getting buffeted around by the current.

She laughed and ran her hand through her hair. Time to go. She looked out across the water, searching for a grouping of stones that would let her cross without having to get wet and found a suitable area but would need to backtrack, so she hopped across the stones back to the embankment. Solaris walked up the creek toward the next set of rocks, listening to the water babble and then stopped in front of her bridge of stones.

She hadn't made it that far yet from the clearing, but she was already feeling better. She reminded herself that once she was at the cliff, she would be able to see open sky and that would make her feel better. The darkness around her was only temporary. She glanced back the way she came and then looked forward again. *I should keep pushing forward.*

Solaris eyed the string of large water stones and decided it was safe enough to try. If she fell in, the temperature wasn't cold enough to be life threatening, but it would make her miserable until she dried off. She hopped across the first couple sets of stones and then paused. A few stones away was another single strand of the water grass she saw earlier. It was bent over just like the one she saw before. Strange that only a single blade would grow.

She watched it bobbing in the water, swaying with the current. *Are you really going to freak out over a piece of grass, Solaris? Wait, did it move closer? Oh, no!*

Solaris stepped back slow, letting her foot

find the previous rock. The blade of grass was moving against the current. *Oh, shit! Oh, shit! It's not grass*. She watched it bob up and down and then she noticed its pattern. It wasn't bobbing with the current; it was probing the tops of the rocks, searching. She didn't need to see anymore. Solaris spun and raced across the stones, her feet landing true, bounding back to the embankment. As she landed on the beach, she heard an eruption of displaced water and frantic splashing. Solaris scrambled up and over the side of the embankment, glancing back as she kept her forward momentum.

Slithering across the water was a giant insect worm with a thousand, many jointed legs. Half of its body stood erect as it rushed across the surface towards her. On the upright end—on its segmented belly—was a vertical slit for a mouth filled with needle sharp teeth. The jointed legs not used for running were spread open in anticipation of grabbing its prey.

Solaris redirected her attention forward and focused on reaching the clearing. She followed the trail of looped moss clumps, pushing her body as hard as it could go. Behind her, she could hear the creature closing in, gargling and clicking with excitement. As she ran, she tried to think of a way to shake the creature, but no flash of brilliance came. Instead, she started weaving in close to the trees, in and out, crisscrossing as she went. Solaris was rewarded by the sound of the creature bouncing off of several trees. The interference wasn't much, but she knew it could buy her a little time, and that might make all the difference.

She kept pushing, driving her legs until they burned. She knew she was almost there and refused to let herself concentrate on the pain in her side or how the air was stinging her lungs. *Not much longer. Come on!*

The first glimpses of light pierced the darkness, and her spirits lifted until she saw something else in front of her. The creature was shuffling across the ground sniffing at a dangle of moss she had looped. It had an abnormally large head with multiple tusks protruding from a short snout. Dark, muddy fur coated its body, and long, tentacle appendages fanned out from the top of its back. They moved through the air like snakes and grabbed at the moss that she had touched earlier, probing for her scent.

Solaris quickly formulated a plan as she heard the insect monster close in behind her. She opted for the most direct route—up and over. She made her way toward the tentacle creature, keeping a tree between them so it couldn't see her coming. Just before she ran straight into the tree, she altered her course to the right, pushed off the side of the trunk, and hurtled herself toward the beast. It flinched as Solaris appeared and released a high-pitched warble. She managed to slap the only tentacle close to her out of the way and hit the ground with a roll.

As she tumbled across the ground, she heard the creature continue to warble in her direction, then there was the sound of two bodies colliding. She looked up and found that the insect worm had collided with the tentacle monster, and they were rolling across the foliage, biting and clawing at each other. The fight didn't last long, as the insect worm wrapped itself around the beast and bit it repeatedly in the throat with its giant mandibles.

Solaris looked around and realized she was in the clearing and kept sliding backwards, making her way deeper into the field. She tried not to draw attention to herself as she rose to her feet and walked backwards. The insect worm kept its thousand legs wrapped around the beast until Solaris crossed the energy barrier. After she passed through the invisible dome, the monster lifted its head and waggled it sole antennae, probing the air. Then it latched onto the carcass of the beast and dragged it into the darkness of the black forest.

CHAPTER 7

A couple hours passed, and after the fourth nearly fatal attempt to escape the woods, she decided Bakuun was telling the truth. Solaris crossed the field and made her way straight to the guardian. She marched through the floating obelisks, passed the uprooted tree he had thrown earlier, and stopped when she reached the little hill he sat on.

Scattered at the base of his hill were thousands of skeletons. Several mounds of bones had grown so large, they were small hills themselves —vegetation grew across them, and birds made nests where they found skulls large enough to house them.

She stopped next to a large rib cage—half buried in the dirt—with a vine growing up one of the spines. She looked out at the skeletons strewn across the area. Most of them looked like animals he must have eaten—some of them were still fresh as she could see rotting skin and meat on more than a few. There were also skulls in the shape of a fah'dienh head, but she tried not to look at those.

He sat in the darkness on his boulder, a hand propped on a knee, leaning in toward her. "I see you found a couple of those that howl and prowl."

Solaris clenched her teeth and took in a breath. "I'm still here."

"Yes, you are. Good that you came back before you proved me correct. Are you ready to talk now?"

"Speak, Bakuun. I'm listening." She wasn't going back into the woods. As much as she hated to admit it, he was right. Her next trip out there might be her last. She would need to figure out another way out.

"Give up this idea you're going to bring them back. You're not. They are gone."

She didn't want to argue with him. She would just have to investigate the possibility of bringing her family back at some other point. "Okay, Bakuun. I hear your warning. If I leave here will I be able to come back? Will I be able to use a different gate?"

"I don't know."

"How do you not know? Aren't you a gate guardian?"

"I guard this gate, but I mostly eat these ugly things running around. I piss where you're standing, and I shit over there. I guess I've been doing that now for a couple thousand years. A lot has changed since then, and I don't get to see much."

Solaris didn't respond immediately. She thought about what he said and found it ironic that he could be so powerful and be so ignorant. *I guess even magic has its limits.* She may never figure out how to bring them back, but she sure as hell could go after the man that murdered her family. *I don't know how, but I'm going to kill him.* "Okay, Bakuun. How do I get back to my world? I have unfinished business," she asked, clenching her fists.

"Indeed. I do have an answer for that and even better, I could help but...," it said and raised an open hand into the air.

Solaris's surprise got the better of her, and she let a huff escape before she asked, "You want something?" *I knew it. He does want something from me. That's why he let me live,* she thought.

"Well yes, but there are complications. That pretty piece of jewelry digging into your chest makes the situation—eh—problematic. But if you give me what I want, I will give you what you want. And what I want is for just a piece of me to leave here. This," it said and beat on its chest. "Cannot leave this place. My body has been bound here for a long—long time. I've been sitting here on this damned rock, alone with my memories... and my hunger. But it has dawned on me that your situation provides a unique opportunity for both of us."

Solaris looked at the shadowy figure as it swayed beyond the trees. She watched the creature watch her for a moment and then asked, "What did you do, Bakuun? Why were you bound to this place?"

It laughed again, deep and loud, sending birds into the sky. "I lived," he growled. "I was honest with myself. True to my nature, but there are those who don't appreciate that. The Seven Hands...they believe themselves better than me. They feel I should have no opportunity to be myself and fear me, and so I am damned forever...maybe. Unless, I'm accepted by a pure soul, not tainted by the darkness that infects this world. Unless, I'm embraced by another. You can carry a seed to be reborn far from here. Not this, but this," he said, raising a hand first to his chest and then a finger to his temple.

Solaris swallowed. "Do you deserve freedom, Bakuun?"

He paused long enough for the young woman to become uncomfortable before Bakuun responded. "To deserve is such a heavy and pretentious word, don't you think? So subjective. Do you deserve to breathe air? Do you deserve to sleep? Do you deserve to leave here?"

"Yes. I have to return," she shouted.

"Why?" he questioned, the word was deep and echoed through the dark forest.

"I…I need to stop someone."

"If you're going to say something, then say what you mean. You mean, you want to kill someone."

"Yes, Bakuun. I want to kill the bastard that murdered my family," she said, but as it rolled off her tongue, her stomach turned. *No, he deserves it.*

Bakuun shifted on his rock and crossed his arms. "Some would tell you that path only leads to destruction, and it won't bring you comfort. Between you and me, I think they are full of shit. They are self-righteous assholes who can think like that so long as nothing bad happens to them. But the moment it does, who do they come to? They come to me, girl. They come to me, because I understand what life is, and I understand how to take it. But you…how exactly are you going to do that? He sent you here, did he not? Killed your family and almost killed you."

"No," she screamed. "I…I killed myself."

He huffed with disbelief. "You committed suicide, so…if you go back now, how exactly are you going to kill him when you were too weak to do it before?"

"I don't know, I'll figure it out, and…I have this now," she said and placed her hand over the Key of Skurien.

"Figure it out?" it sneered. "And you think you will because you've done so well so far… You don't even know what it is, much less how to use its power. It takes years of practice to understand deep magic girl. I've known mages that were apprentices for longer than you'll live."

"Then tell me," she shouted. "Tell me how to kill him!"

"No…I don't think I will," said Bakuun as he sat up straight. "*But…*we can kill this man together. That, I will grant you."

"How? I thought you were bound here?"

"My body, but not my mind. Not my essence. As a vessel, you can take a piece of me back and call upon it when you need me. I'll take care of the rest."

Solaris brought her hands up and held her stomach, fighting the urge to throw up. "And all I have to do is accept you? What does that mean?"

"Yes. Just accept me, and let me in. I'll just squeeze into a small corner of your soul. You would hardly even notice I'm there. For that, I promise to help you get home and end the man that is responsible for the death of your family," it said.

"I...I don't—,"

"What is there to debate? You want out, and you want him dead. There is one way to do this! And that way is through me and me alone," it growled and stood up.

She paused for a moment, feeling a sense of doubt surfacing in her mind but then pushed it away. *I have no choice. He's right. If I go back without a plan or help, the captain will just kill me or worse.* "What do I need to do to accept you?" she said darting her eyes away, trying to ignore the queasiness in her stomach.

Bakuun raised one arm to the sky and stretched his clawed talons wide. As he did so she saw him smile and noticed the whiteness of his canines piercing the darkness surrounding his body —glowing like hungry, ivory daggers of malice.

A brilliant white flash of lightning came down from the sky and struck the ground before Solaris. In answer to the strike, a light green mist rose out from beneath the ground. It first flowed over the grass, pooling at her feet, and then it swirled up and around her body like an ethereal snake and condensed into a ball directly in front of her face. The green mist swirled and pulsed with soft green light, expanding and contracting in size. The longer she stared at the wisp, the more she could feel her resistance fading. It called to her. Unfamiliar sounds came from within, and whispers formed, tickling her ears with promises.

We can avenge them, Solaris. Let us help. Let us in. Let us lend you our power.

"All you have to do is say...I accept you Bakuun...and then breathe. That's it."

"What is this?" she asked staring at the mist.

"It doesn't matter, and it won't hurt you. But rest assured, it is the only deal you get from me and it's the best deal you'll get. No one can help you the way I can."

"How do I know you'll—,"

"I'll keep my end of the bargain? You don't," it snapped. "If we talked about this long enough, I know you could conjure all sorts of insidious scenarios of where this turns out bad for you. The truth is I want to use you, and you want to use me. That's just called a deal, and I really don't want you to walk off into those woods again because I know of twelve creatures prowling the perimeter right now that will tear you apart. They're just waiting for you. All that commotion earlier has drawn them here. I don't want you to die because who knows how long it will be before another Mestagorii stumbles upon my gate, if ever. This deal is mutually beneficial to both of us, so what'll it be? The devil you know or the devil you don't?"

127

Solaris looked at her immediate surroundings. She traced the edge of the woods, listening to the unfamiliar howls and watched red eyes move along the edge and then disappear into the darkness. She knew there would be more consequences to accepting his deal than he let on, just as much as she knew if she stepped foot in those dark woods again, she was as good as dead.

It's okay, Solaris. We will take care of you, said the wisp.

Images of her family passed through her mind. Birthdays. Dinners. Vacations. Things that never would come to pass.

"Okay," she whispered.

Bakuun tilted his head slightly, "What was that?"

She planted her feet and stared him down. "I accept you, Bakuun," she screamed.

Solaris scarcely processed what happened next. The green mist pressed into her, forcing its way in through her nose and mouth and filled every portion of her body. The smell of dank moss and rich earth filled her nostrils and then the world went black again. At some point, her mind came back together, and she realized she was falling again but upward this time.

And fast.

CHAPTER 8

Solaris awakened and gasped. She clawed at the ground, fighting through the burning sensation as it chewed its way through her chest. She could feel the key burying deeper into her heart, grinding against her sternum and ribs in the process.

All the men turned from a dead comrade and looked down at Solaris writhing on the ground.

"I thought she was dead," whispered one of the men.

The captain said, "Well...I'll be damned," and walked over to her, pushing one of the men out of the way.

He reached down and grabbed a fistful of her hair. "Does it hurt? I hope it does. You cost me a fuckin' for—," he said, but she cut him off with an ear-piercing howl. He released her and took a step back and then another.

Solaris's body started convulsing, and the hair from her head shot out and whipped in all directions. *What's happening to me?* Energy raced through her body, and she released another howl.

Then a noise like boulders grinding against each other exploded outward, and gusts of torrential force whipped at the group from all angles. The pendant embedded in her chest began to glow pink, and soft light slowly engulfed her entire body as she levitated free of the ground. First, she was limp, and then her muscles contracted as she felt the presence of another being within her mind. Around her, the large roza formations began to glow, and long trails of intertwining pink light swam through the air and merged with her body.

Solaris floated freely in the air, defying gravity, her muscles contracting and releasing out of control. She became disoriented because of the pain, but she could still sense the presence of the being. For a moment, she didn't know what it was or what it wanted, but then a jolt of pain shocked a memory forth from the deep recesses of her mind.

The vivid memory was one from her childhood. She saw her grandmother, grey haired and smiling, looking over her as she lay in bed. The old woman bent over and gave her a kiss. Then her grandmother sung a song. After the song was ended, the old woman said, "Remember, the heart, that is the guardian's lock...And this," said the woman, "is the key." She was holding up the pink pendant. "Do not forget it."

I remember! Then she wanted something else. *Help me, Bakuun! Kill them all!*

In response, the vision vanished from her eyes, but the violent gusts didn't—they multiplied. The wind whipped so mightily, it drove most of the humans to drop to their knees, and the few slavers who didn't were hammered back until they were blasted over the edge, disappearing forever into the darkness below.

The pink circulating mist faded away, leaving black tendrils of mist lashing out from her body. The dark tentacles pulled the bit out of her mouth and then whipped wildly, groping nearby roza stones and trees before letting them go to continue probing anything else nearby. As the pain intensified, so did the number of tendrils and their ferocity. One of the humans stood up against the wind and turned from her to escape. As he marched away, one of the black tendrils seized his body, wrapping all the way down from his neck to his ankle. He was jerked high into the air and then slammed into the ground before being whipped upward toward Solaris again.

The stunned brigand batted at the tendrils like a drunk but could not find anything physical to grip. He clawed desperately at the ethereal substance, trying to stop its penetration, but his fingers passed through the darkness as if it were smoke. The dark energy swarmed his body, solidifying and misting as the need arose to work the man into position. The seething blackness flowed over him and poured into all the cracks of his defensive shell. His armor rippled unnaturally before entire plates were blasted off his body into the night, piece-by-piece, until only clothing was left. After the last of the armor was ripped away, the living darkness separated into four distinct tendrils and bound all of the man's limbs, stretching him in all directions, forcing him within reach of Solaris. As the man drifted toward her, Bakuun's voice pierced her mind with one command.

Take him!

While she knew exactly what to do, she didn't know why she was doing it, but her ignorance didn't hinder her from acting. Solaris wrapped her arms around the man from behind and pulled him in close. When he touched her body, his body burst into flames, but the heat had no effect on her. He burned, screamed, and then disintegrated into a cloud of green mist. Bakuun's voice came again.

Breathe deep if you want to live.

Solaris pushed all the air from her lungs and then sucked in as large a breath as she could. As she did, the green mist raced into her body, forcing its way in through her mouth and nostrils. She could feel it coursing through her, a cold sensation penetrating her entire being. No sooner had she finished taking in her breath, than a sharp spasm ripped through her muscles. She cycled through unnatural contortions as the pain left her muscles and burrowed deep into her bones. When she couldn't take it any longer, she screamed. Her high-pitched voice cut through the night before quickly deepening into a bottomless roar.

Parts of her body morphed in rapid succession, starting with her knees snapping backwards and her feet melting into three-toed hooves. Her once slender body stretched and grew larger, bones elongated, and new tissue and tendons grew to match the developing skeleton. At first, she looked emaciated and then the muscles began building on top of each—bulking—layer-after-layer. As her muscles rippled into place, her short fingernails grew into coal-black talons, and her soft, tan skin gave way to short cropped, light-brown fur. She had another massive growth spasm and ripped through most of her clothing, leaving it a tattered mess hanging from her body.

Twisted horns exploded from the top of her head and wrapped backwards. Solaris's long black hair fell out in clumps as her mouth protruded into a snout, and her emerald green eyes intensified until they were glowing like green coals.

The beast that was Solaris settled to the ground. She swayed in place as she tried to focus her senses, but she was unable to bring her mind under control. Comprehension surfaced and vanished within seconds. Sounds were foreign. The feel of her body was alien. Was she running from something? No...she had to fight! She scanned the area but only made out blurs. Some moved and others didn't. It took her several seconds to realize the moving shapes were humans, and half as long to understand they were running from her. She staggered toward one but then stopped to lean on a tree as she nearly lost her balance. The tree protested loudly against her weight, but it held. *What's happening to me?*

As she watched, another human appeared between the stationary blurs, and she seized the opportunity. *I have to stop them!* Solaris moved forward, straightening as she went, but as she planted her feet they gave way. She lurched right and crashed into a tree, heard the trunk splinter and then the tree toppled. Though she couldn't see him, she could make out the sound of a man screaming until the tree ended his existence. Solaris moved along the fallen tree, using it as a guide and to balance. She reached forward to move a branch out of her way and froze. Where her hand should have been was a clawed, monstrous thing; she willed it to close and watched the taloned fingers obey. Before she could react to this, there came a loud series of sharp, high-pitched sounds and then pain leapt up her backside. She bellowed and pushed off the earth and stumbled forward in a leaping motion, bouncing off large trees as she went.

You need to calm your mind and focus your will, girl, shouted Bakuun in her mind.

Staying on her feet while moving was proving to be beyond difficult. After several attempts at running, she collapsed to the ground and began crawling. Not only did her limbs feel weak, but they were sluggish. Despite this, she willed her body to move forward, but she wasn't able to cover much ground. Then the blurs came back. Several suddenly raced past her and took position directly in her path. Just as she made up her mind to charge through them, a series of flashes erupted. She flinched, expecting to feel pain again, but they did not fire upon her. Light blue streaks struck the ground in front of her, kicking up bits of earth and chunks of seared wood into the air. She veered left and the firing came again, throwing up dirt and debris into her path. She abruptly stopped, and her feet flew out from underneath her. *They're hemming me in,* she thought and rolled over. Before she could react to this she felt something slip around the base of her arm and jerk her forward; she lost her balance and fell to the ground. Her head crashed against a large boulder, and the memory of the captain executing her father burst into her mind. As she heard the shot echo again for the second time that night, she roared, "No!"

Then something else grabbed her wrist and pulled hard, so her large body was stretched across the ground. She roared and jerked her arm toward her chest. To her amazement, a man flipped out of the brush and crashed into her. He hit the ground and then sprang to his feet, but before he could get away she slashed through the air and struck him. Her blow sent him careening through the air as if gravity had suddenly relinquished its hold on him. As she tracked his movement, her vision became sharp again, and she watched him smack headlong into a boulder. He tumbled to the ground and moved no more. *Die! All of you!*

Solaris snatched her head around to see what gripped her leg—a yellow rope bound her to a nearby tree. The rope was wound around the tree and ended in the hands of four human men. She twisted her body to reach for the rope around her ankle and collapsed to the ground again. With her back to them, the pirates scurried in and slipped another rope around her free wrist. After feeling the bite of the new binding, she turned back, lashed out at an armored man and missed as the human rolled away from her clawed embrace.

The men surrounded her, ramming the snare poles into her body. She tried frantically to free herself, but there were just too many. They beat her with their poles and sticks until they had her positioned how they wanted her. Within minutes, they had her other free limbs caught and tightened down with ropes.

Solaris roared and pulled, but she wasn't strong enough to overcome the men holding the restraints. She could feel a new strength flowing through her body, but she was unaware of how to tap into it. Now, there were at least six men on each rope, and each rope was wrapped around a massive tree. As she lay prostrate on the ground, several more men came up to her and tried slipping a black cargo net underneath her massive body. When it wouldn't slide underneath, someone shouted, "Tighten down until she clears the ground. Ready, now, boys...heave!"

The ropes tightened in all directions, and pain ripped through all of her limbs as they were stretched.

"Ho," shouted the human again, and the ropes held. The speaker paused to give his men time to reset and then said, "Heave."

The ropes pulled at her joints, and she was sure her feet and hands were close to being pulled apart. She bellowed as the pain forced all other thoughts from her mind. The men held her there as the net was snatched underneath. After it cleared, she was lowered back down to the ground, but the ropes were held tight enough so she couldn't bend any of her limbs.

She moaned as the wind picked up around

her. A loud roaring noise came from above. She glanced up and was immediately blinded by flood lights shining down on her position. She turned her head away. *No! No! This isn't supposed to be happening!* Dust blew into her eyes, and she closed them, but not for long. *Bakuun where are you?* She sensed someone had approached, and she reopened her eyes to find a pair of black boots in front of her face. She stared at the boots until the human squatted down in front of her. It was the captain.

"You still in there, girl?" he asked and ran his hand along one of her antlers.

Solaris lurched forward and snapped at the man.

He nodded without even flinching. "I'll take that as a yes...wow," he said and ran his hand over the top of her head.

She turned her head to bite at him again, but he spun and then brought his knee down behind the back of her head. At the same time, he grabbed both of her antlers and twisted until the side of her face was pressed into the ground. She growled and snorted, sending large clouds of dust and dried leaves into the air.

"I have to admit that this took me by surprise. I've been to a few different worlds, and *never* have I seen anything like you. And you are absolutely beautiful. I mean it," he said. As he ran a hand across the side of her face, she watched the space craft slowly descend and lower its cargo hatch. The vehicle settled in a natural clearing close enough to throw heat in her direction. She kept her eyes closed until the hot air ceased to blow across her face.

"Bring the drop cords for the cargo net," he said.

Half-a-dozen men poured out of the belly of the vehicle, each pulling a black cable with a clasp. The cables were fed from swiveling pulley arms at the edge of the cargo opening; they were massive, industrial-sized mechanisms. The men ran to her position and hooked the clasps to various points on the cargo net underneath her. After hooking the clasps, the men jerked upward on the cord, and this caused a cylindrical fastener to sheave the clasp in place. The captain patted her head and then stepped off and away from her snarling maw.

"You know...I just had this net especially made for my tracker. You remember the tracker. It's my pet that ripped your brother apart. Anyway, the net was designed to haul its big ass out of the jungle. He was always running off after a hunt, but I digress. While you were playing with your brother's dead body, I was lamenting the fact that you killed my beast, and I wouldn't get a chance to try out my new toy. And then later on, when you were wallowing on the ground, it struck me that it would do a damn fine job on you too."

"Goooo," she groaned. She found it was very difficult to vocalize her words. Her new mouth wasn't the best at articulation.

"What?" he laughed.

"Let go," she growled and tried the bonds holding her, but the struggle only served to tighten the knots further. She winced as the bonds burned into her flesh. In exasperation, Solaris flexed her clawed fingers and then dug them into the ground wishing the human was in reach.

He looked down at her and smiled with only one side of his mouth turning up. The captain held his gaze for a moment, looked toward the craft and then back to her before saying, "I'll tell you what. Since you made a deal with me, I'll make one with you. If you can get free of my net, I'll tell me boys to stand down. Let you pass," he said and chuckled. "Hell, I'll even drop you off wherever you want to go. How about that? How does that sound?"

She didn't say anything. She knew he was lying, only toying with her. He obviously knew she wouldn't be able to escape. She wasn't sure what he had up his sleeve, but she knew it wouldn't benefit her.

"Ready?" he asked and raised his hand. "As soon as I drop my hand, my men are going to let go of the ropes. And we'll just see who's the boss.

Fah'dienh magic or human ingenuity."

The look on his face told her everything she needed to know. He was trying to prove something. Whether it was to her, his men, or himself, she wasn't sure. Solaris readied herself, furrowing her brow and growling. She locked eyes with the captain. A new, more powerful and overwhelming urge was rushing through her mind. She tensed her muscles and flexed her fingers. His armored ensemble had a glaring weak spot—he wore no helmet. If he gave her a second, that's all she would need. Let them do what they wanted to her—she was going to kill the bastard first!

He dropped his hand, and the ropes tied to her limbs went slack. In that split second, she caught herself, coiled her muscles, and then sprang. All of her focus was upon the man, and she watched as his eyes went wide. Watched as she recognized the look of fear in his eyes. The admission before death—he had been wrong, and his own arrogance had hastened his demise. Her giant, clawed hand came down and then twisted to the side as the black net whipped around her body. As it snatched her from her feet, it spun at the same time and tightened down until she was bound so tight she could barely breathe. Solaris crashed into the earth, fighting against the net and bellowing. She pressed against the net but couldn't get her hand through as the holes in the netting were too small. Only seconds later, the world began to spin as the drop cords began pulling her toward the shuttle.

"It's a carbon fiber weave," said the captain as he walked beside her. Whatever was pulling her along was slow enough for him to walk leisurely and talk to her. Slow enough for him to strut. "Damn near indestructible. It also appears to be well suited for catching young women that can turn into monsters. Wasn't sure if you noticed that or not."

"I'll kill you," she huffed.

"Well...that's not the first time I've heard that, but it might be the last. Someone is going to pay me a fortune for you. But look at the bright side. You probably won't be used for your body now. Doesn't that make you happy?" he asked. "Course...a lab might be a worse fate. I guess it depends on how you look at it."

Movement caught Solaris's eye, and she gazed into the belly of the craft. A man was on the far end, and he was frantically slicing his hand through the air. As he did so, different colored lights played across his face. From her angle, she couldn't tell what held his attention; she saw only the flashing projecting onto his face. He stopped mid-slice and became very still as a red light blinked in and out of existence. He didn't study the red light long before he bolted around his station, knocking a crate off a bench in the process.

Tools and trash tumbled to the ground, nearly causing the man to trip and fall, but he kept his balance. The human sprinted toward their location and slid to a stop just beyond the cargo bay doors. He cupped his hands around his mouth. "Watch out! They're here! Ru—," shouted the man before his warning was ended. A dark flash struck him in the neck, and blood spurted from the wound and raced down the length of a thick and straight arrow embedded just under his chin. He clasped desperately, as if trying to stem the gush of blood and then dove face first into the ground. Protruding from his neck was a strong and straight arrow with yellow and green fletching. Solaris's heart soared. She would recognize that type of arrow anywhere. It was the same kind the men made in her grandmother's village. Urokos. The Tree People had come.

"Secure the cargo," screamed the captain.

Solaris watched several men break away from the group and charge toward the vehicle. When they were only meters away from the entrance, dozens of arrows rained down upon them. Many of the arrows bounced off the humans' armor, but just enough found a weak spot between the plates. The human men fell to the ground in anguish, groping at the shafts embedded into their flesh. Arrows protruded from the gaps near their necks, underneath their arms, behind their knees, and near their waistlines.

The captain drew his pistol and shouted, "They're in the goddamn trees! Keep going and light-em up!"

The pirates created a semi-circle in front of Solaris, continuing their movement forward as they opened fire into the upper branches. Bright blue beams of light streaked through the air toward where the arrows had originated. The dark jungle came alive with aqua colored light as the humans sent a deluge of energy beams through the trees. Within seconds, the canopy was riddled with orange glowing rings of ember and pockets of fire.

"Cease firing," shouted the captain. "Stop firing, god damnit! Conserve ammo." She watched him scan the upper branches of the trees and then the ground. Solaris scanned where she thought he was looking and felt a surge of relief. There were no fah'dineh bodies on the ground. She hoped the humans hadn't hit anyone. Solaris brought her attention away from the men and looked at the net binding her. *I have to get free of this,* she thought. She squirmed until she was able to slide her arms further up her body. While her hands were too big to fit through the holes, her fingers were not. She fed them through the gaps and grasped the closest clasp. She pressed against the metal sphere trying to pry it loose, but it held fast. She looked at the humans again to make sure no one was watching her.

"Yamisee," shouted a voice from the jungle. It was both a question and a command. This utterance sent an unfamiliar emotion racing through her system. It grabbed her attention and sent her thoughts reeling and something else struggled to surface. Something foreign. She felt her mind go foggy for a moment and then she regained control.

Then behind them another fah'dienh responded, "Yamisee!" Shivers ran up and down her body.

"What the fuck are they saying?" asked one of the brigands.

"I don't know," whispered the captain. "Just keep your fingers on the triggers. It's not much further now."

"We're not going to make it. Fuck," stammered another man. "They're fucking everywhere, man!"

"Shut your mouth, Jones! Keep your eyes open, and we'll get out of this," said a different human.

"Everybody shut up," said the captain. "Listen."

Then from all directions, the warriors began to chant in unison, "Yamisee...Yamisee...Yamisee!" Solaris recognized the word but couldn't remember what it meant. It was a word from the old tongue. Even still, as the chant drew on, she felt an emotion begin to stir deep within her. It lulled her eyes to close, and she felt herself gently rocking to the rhythm of the chant. The word was more than a word. She could feel the calling flowing into her, warming her like a hug from her mom on a cold night. The chanting begged her—compelled her to act. Solaris both wanted and felt obligated to join the fah'dienh. Escape was no longer an option. She was compelled to help them. She had to help them. She *must* help.

The men were huddled together closely and traced their guns through the treetops. Red laser dots danced across the broad leaves of the canopy, but they failed to locate anything worth bringing down. The mercenaries held loose positions around her as they inched closer toward the craft. Any noise or slight movement in the trees brought their guns up. Solaris could smell their sweat through the suits. Smell their breath —their unwashed bodies. She hadn't been aware of it before, but the smell was very pungent to her. As she studied this new aspect of her senses, she became aware that there were other creatures moving about their position. Although it was faint, she could hear the protesting whisper of leaves branches were brushed aside, the loose rustle of clothing against skin, the low twang of a bow string getting caught on foliage. More from some new instinct than anything else, she closed her eyes to focus her full attention on what was making the noises. She closed her mind off to all senses, except sound. Solaris pushed away the sounds of her captors stomping through the leaves. Shut away the sound of their clinking armor and hissing guns. Isolated the electronic whirrings coming from the craft. After separating the noises, there arose a void in her mind for something else. Not a void. An...un-thing. It was like standing in an empty room but feeling the presence of someone else. The same way you could both feel and hear a person all in one sense.

An unexpected knowing planted the knowledge of something large in the jungle directly in front of her. Waiting. No. There were several large creatures she felt more than smelt or heard. And then she could hear the captain exhale like his breath was a gust of wind. It was deep and became rhythmic. She opened her eyes and found the captain next to her, gazing at the treetops. It was then she realized the breathing she heard was from more than one being. It wasn't the captain.

The sound of leather slapping a hide made her jolt, and several of the humans turned to look down at her. Then the screams of birds pierced the night as they took flight.

"They come," she whispered.

A loud crash came from the jungle, then the crack of a tree splintering from force. As the crashes became louder, a low rumble could be felt and heard from their standpoint. As they watched, a glint of metal flashed in the darkness of the jungle, and the humans whirled in the direction of the gleam.

"Burn them!" growled the captain.

"Aye," responded a man next to them. He hopped in front of the line of mercenaries and pulled an oblong sphere from his vest. The human pressed his thumb against the device and flung it out into the darkness. As the device came down, it burst open and jettisoned several hissing, red-blinking balls. A foul-smelling gas reached Solaris's nostrils before a spark ignited the fuel, and a ball of flame rose several stories high. The heat from the explosion rolled over them like a summer wind on a star's surface. Solaris closed her eyes and roared as the scalding air singed the hairs across her face and shoulder.

Then came the moment of stillness—a time of breath holding. The jolt of the explosion caused her to lose her connection with the others. The flames curled and bloomed upward into the black of night, creating an orange wall of pain and rage. She counted as she waited, feeling hope slipping—knowing her people were outmatched.

But then a massive yhsaril with a spear-wielding fah'dienh on its back emerged from the flames at full gallop. Fire be damned! The grey creature had a large, flat, armored head and tree trunks for legs. It seemed to be ignoring the blood pouring from several holes in its head fin and the fire licking up its sides. After the creature cleared the flames, several more yhsaril followed suit. The humans fired desperately into the charging war beasts, but there were too many, and they were already upon them. Solaris watched in horror and relief as the group bore down on them.

"Run," shouted the captain. And they did, but not fast enough. The first yhsaril reached the men and plowed straight through their ranks. Several humans were trampled and thrown into the air as it barreled through, swinging its massive head like a battering ram. Another followed close to the first's path, and to Solaris's dismay, the captain jumped out of the way, narrowly avoiding being trampled to death. The third yhsaril skimmed the edge of the men, but the warrior on its back brought a spear down on a tall human still firing into the warriors. The spear found its mark between the man's helmet and collarbone, taking him off his feet. As he fell backwards, his death grip fired the weapon in his hand and haphazardly issued blue beams of light, blowing a hole through one of his comrades and taking the head off of a fah'dienh warrior.

Solaris suddenly struck something hard and realized she had reached the cargo plate. She rocked back and forth frantically, trying to free herself as the machine dragged her into the belly of the craft. She froze as she saw the others inside. Several women were pressed against the bars of their cages, some with their arms through the slits groping wildly into the air and screaming. She watched them as a sickening feeling begin to settle in her gut. One of the women turned to her and gasped, bringing her hand up to her mouth. She immediately reached through the bars of her side wall and grabbed the girl next to her. Wild-eyed, the girl turned to see who was grabbing her and —in the process—noticed Solaris. She too gasped and shouted for the others to look. All of the women turned their gazes upon her in amazement and then the original girl who saw her shouted, "Yamisee!" It was then she remembered what the word meant. *Green Mother? They think I'm the Green Mother?*

An older woman toward the front screamed, "Yamisee," and the men charging the cargo hatch responded back with a battle cry. A new commotion caught her attention, and she looked back toward the humans. Several of the mercenaries took up position on the edge of the docking plate and opened fire into her people. More humans charged deeper into the craft and disappeared down corridors beyond her sight.

"Get off the fucking ground," shouted the captain. He was standing next to his men firing his handgun into the crowd of warriors swelling at the edge. Right on cue, the entire craft rumbled and shook violently. A loud whining noise issued and then two large thumps boomed outside. One-by-one, the humans ran out of ammo and dropped their rifles to the ground. For each rifle they dropped, two fah'dienh warriors appeared in the opening with a weapon in hand. Ammo depleted, the humans pulled their knives and metal sticks out. Humans and fah'dienh screamed and engaged each other in hand to hand combat. Knives flashed through the air, and spears were driven home. The humans leveraged their high ground and armor as the fah'dienh capitalized on overwhelming num-bers while executing swift and precise move-ments.

Solaris scanned the mass of writhing mer-cenaries and warriors for the captain. He was on his back and being driven into the corner. The fah'dienh warrior was on top of him and pressing a knife downward toward the human's eye. *Kill him*, she thought. *Do it!* The knife inched closer, and the human turned away as the blade caught his cheek and drew blood. She growled as the smell of his blood hit her nostrils. The captain suddenly jerked to the side and pulled the warrior forward. As the warrior collapsed on top of him, the human kicked one of his legs out and flipped them both over so he was on top.

"No," she bellowed.

In a swift, practiced move, the captain twisted the man's arm, and she could hear the warrior's arm bones snap. The knife fell, and before it struck the ground, the captain had released his grip to bury his thumbs into the fah'dienh man's eye sockets. The warrior screamed and thrashed wildly, but only for a few seconds before he fell still. As soon as he was dead, the captain reached down, grabbed the knife, and then pressed a bloody hand to his throat.

"Why the fuck haven't we taken off?" shouted the captain. He paused as he seemed to contemplate something. It was then Solaris realized he must have some other communication device allowing him to hear what his men were saying. He leapt up from his position. "Skip that shit. Get us off the fucking ground now!" The human looked at Solaris and sneered before diving back into the throng of men at the opening.

The clear artificial lights above went out and were replaced by a bright red spinning light. The shuttle rumbled, and she heard the sound of the propulsion system firing up on both sides of the craft. A speaker overhead blared, "Ignition sequence engaged. Hold on to your asses!" The craft lurched upward, and several men fell out of the cargo hold: fah'dienh and human both. The vehicle continued to ascend and then it violently veered sideways, sending Solaris hurtling left and jerked to a stop as the cords holding her snagged on the pulleys. The overhead speaker blared to life again as a loud siren screeched into the dark night.

There were muffled human sounds and shouting followed by a brief spurt of words. "Somebody get up here! They're inside th—," and then the transmission became distorted and cut out.

She could feel the craft level off and then slowly turn downward as the pull of gravity changed on her body. The vehicle reversed its ascent and began to spiral downwards. Everything not tied down or in a cage went airborne too. The women in the cages screamed as they clutched the bars. The battle continued as combatants were bounced around the cargo bay. Two men slammed into a corner of the craft and then down into the flooring near a set of pulley arms. The warrior desperately clawed at the human for purchase, but as he did, several round objects were wrenched free of the man's armored vest, one of them blinking red. The human screamed, but it wasn't one of fury. The scream ended abruptly with a flash of light and a burst of heat.

The explosion jolted her world, and a side of the jumper blew away, along with one of the rope pullies securing her in place. The view outside cycled between black star strewn sky and the jungle canopy, blue with the light of the moon. Solaris tumbled toward the back of the craft and as she did, the black cords snagged on the remaining industrial pulley and ripped it free of the mounting. The net became slack, and she inadvertently slipped an arm free searching for a handhold. She slid to one side of the craft and then another before hurtling toward the cargo opening, frantically clawing at floor grates with her free arm.

Just as she secured a grip on the grating and stopped her expulsion, something slammed into her back and then securely wrapped around her neck. She watched the outside world spin and wiggled her body to try and free herself from whatever was choking her. In her mind's eye, she imagined a bundle of ropes had come lose and wrapped around her throat. Her only hope was to hang on until they landed and then try and pull them free. The fall seemed to become endless, like the ground had moved out of the way, but she knew they would be crashing any moment. The thing around her neck tightened more, crushing her throat. She desperately wanted to rip it away from her body, but she couldn't let go or she'd risk being jettisoned from the craft. Solaris coughed and gasped for air, her grip losing its strength, as she watched the view outside rotate.

Stars.

Tree tops.

Stars.

A clearing with something burning.

Stars.

The captain's voice in her ear. "See you

on the other side." Pressure built up in her head as something hard squeezed her neck. Her eyes budged in their sockets, and she tried to move her free arm, but it wouldn't respond.

Darkness.

Authors Note

Thanks for reading and don't worry, book two (a full length novel) is coming soon! Early 2021. Please consider leaving a review on Amazon or Goodreads. It's the main way I can recieve feedback to improve my craft and write better stories for you! I welcome all feedback, but hope you loved it!

I'd also love for you to join my mailing list. It's the easiest way for me to let you know when the next book is available. You can signup on my author homepage at http://www.beharnage.com.

Additionally, you can contact or add me on facebook at B.E. Harnage or at contact@beharnage.com.

Made in the USA
Columbia, SC
13 February 2021